Rising. . .with bright new love
Stars. . .that work their own special magic

Poppy woke to find herself sprawled on the floor.

She blinked, focused, then promptly squeezed her eyes shut. 'Stop pretending, Poppy Brown. I know you're awake,' Tom said.

She groaned. He was an apparition. If she stayed very still he'd go away. Then she suddenly found herself allowing the apparition to haul her to her feet—so wobbly that she clutched at his chest for support. But when her fingers encountered warm, hard flesh she flinched. 'You're real!'

'Of course I'm bloody real.' His mouth twisted as he disengaged her hand, holding her away from him. 'And you're as mad as ever!'

One special month, four special authors. Some of the names you might recognise, like Jessica Matthews, whose book this month is also the beginning of a trilogy. Lucy Clark and Jenny Bryant offer their second books, while **Poppy's Passion** *introduces Helen Shelton.*

Rising Stars. . .catch them while you can!

Dear Reader

A man called one Tuesday with letters from London for me. They were wrongly addressed, and he'd been knocking on doors. Once I realised the letters meant **Poppy's Passion** would be published I doubt I made sense.

Even less when I telephoned Harlequin Mills & Boon to explain why I hadn't returned their contract. In a champagne-induced haze now, I do remember shrieking, 'Cockroach!' as one hurtled behind the telephone of the bug-infested flat we'd sadly just leased.

We discovered my manuscript bore my London street number and my Sydney street name—we'd only just moved from London. They were very polite. But faintly wary. They didn't ask why I'd screamed, 'Cockroach!' at them and I didn't try to explain.

'Fact of life,' the pest man said, 'in Sydney.' Along with the glorious weather and cockatoos. Not a lot about insects in romance novels, I've realised. The pest man was attractive, rugged, really. I wonder. . .

Helen Shelton.

POPPY'S PASSION

BY

HELEN SHELTON

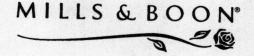

MILLS & BOON®

1907 38000.

First published in Great Britain 1997
Large Print edition 1998
Harlequin Mills & Boon Limited,
Eton House, 18-24 Paradise Road, Richmond,
Surrey TW9 1SR

© Helen Shelton 1997

ISBN 0 263 15412 2

Set in Times 16 on 16 pt. by
Rowland Phototypesetting Limited
Bury St Edmunds, Suffolk

17-9803-54609

Printed and bound in Great Britain
by The Ipswich Book Company Limited, Ipswich

CHAPTER ONE

POPPY swerved her battered Honda into the Royal National Hospital's car park. Spotting a large area thankfully still free of vehicles, she raced towards it, screeched to a stop, grabbed the plastic bag that held her pens and stethoscope and hurtled towards the hospital, her long red hair spilling behind her like a fiery veil.

'Hurry, hurry,' she panted, shoving aside the clear plastic door that guarded the entrance. Inside—abruptly—she skidded to a halt. Her breath coming in quick, panicky puffs, she scanned the green arrowed signs on the wall of the deserted corridor which should have told her where to find Casualty. It was less than three months since her job interview but she'd been very nervous, too nervous to remember now where the department had been.

X-Ray and main entrance to the left, wards everywhere, Maternity and Path Lab upstairs, McDonald's—? Poppy blinked. McDonald's? There was a sign for a hamburger restaurant but none for the casualty department? She knew that the hospital prided itself on its use of private enterprise to increase heath-care funds but something was wrong with their priorities here. What if she was a desperately ill patient with a. . .horrible wound? Did McDonald's offer bandages with its French fries? Would enjoying a good hamburger be adequate compensation for bleeding to death?

And where was everybody? Poppy twisted her head, scanning the empty corridor and stairwells and feeling the seconds tick over as she hesitated, increasingly alarmed by the eerie silence that surrounded her.

'It's like the *Mary Celeste*,' she whispered.

There'd been hundreds of cars in the car parks so somewhere there had to be people. . .but where?

The hairs on the backs of her arms stood up as her mind flicked through the possibilities. Nerve toxin in the air-conditioning unit? Cyanide in the water supply? Mass alien abductions? Ronald McDonald—cannibalistic slaughterer?

'You're tired,' she muttered feebly. 'You're *very* tired and you read too much science fiction.' Both of those things were true but neither seemed especially reassuring. 'Get a grip on yourself!' she muttered, firmer now. 'You haven't had a scrap of sleep in two days and you're not thinking rationally. This is just an ordinary hospital.'

But it didn't feel like an ordinary hospital.

'Find a ward,' she told herself. 'The staff will tell you where to find Casualty.' A glance at the old-fashioned watch which adorned her pale, goose-bumped arm reminded her how late she was. 'Hurry.

'And stop talking to yourself.' She made for the stairs and for Green Ward, which a sign told her she'd find on the first floor. 'People will think you're a lunatic.'

But finding Green Ward didn't help. It was on the first floor, and it was very green—walls, bedspreads, furniture, curtains, floor—but the one thing it lacked was anybody to tell her where to go. No patients, no staff—nothing but green things and the overwhelming impression that the place had been abruptly abandoned, bedside tables still strewn with chocolates and grapes and bottles of half-consumed lemon barley water.

Poppy backed out of the ward, clutching the green wall for support—her mouth dry, her legs quivering. 'It really is the *Mary Celeste*,' she breathed. 'The *Mary Celeste* of the NHS.'

She was the only thing left alive in this building and whatever had happened here had happened suddenly.

Whirling back to the stairs, she tore down— taking the steps two then three at a time and jumping the last set in her desperation to reach the corridor exit and safety.

She didn't see the man coming towards the door until it was too late to stop herself cannoning into what felt like a chest made of concrete. For one dazed moment she stared numbly up at his face, then her head spun and just before she collapsed into a horrified faint at Tom Grainger's feet she screamed, 'Alien! You're an alien!'

When Poppy left Oxford to start her first year at London's St John's College of Medicine her brother, Jeremy, asked Tom Grainger to keep an eye on her.

The two men had attended medical school and later trained as housemen together and now, although working as surgical registrars in different parts of the country, they remained good friends; it was natural for Jeremy to share his worries about his little sister.

'You know what her upbringing's been like,' he said. 'Girls-only schools and no boyfriends. The only males she's ever met are my friends.'

'And you're worried she'll get to med school and want to make up for lost time,' Tom suggested lightly.

'Worried she'll forget to concentrate on her exams,' Jeremy admitted.

'I'll watch out for her.' Tom knew how hard Poppy had worked to get her place at St John's. 'She'll be all right.'

But Poppy—a bemused, dreamy young student, away from home and among strangers for the first time in her life—had had a crush on her brother's handsome friend for years. To have Tom's attention at last—his guidance around the college and hospital and the invitations to dinner at his flat, which came as soon as he discovered that she was living on fast food and instant pot noodles—was electrifying.

Within weeks she decided that he was the most exciting man in the world and that she loved him passionately.

Lacking experience of love but a voracious reader, she turned to books to learn, and devoured romantic novels as if they were biscuits.

Although Tom never kissed or touched her, although at times she caught him watching her as if puzzled by the muddled chaos she tended to create in her life, she understood from her reading that deep inside he loved her too— loved her passionately, but was in awe of her innocence. He was an orderly, organised person and he was devoted to his work so a great passion would overwhelm that calm life—little wonder he fought his ardour.

But this was the late 1980s and her college was full of modern girls. Their stories of romantic and sexual exploits broadened the knowledge Poppy gained from her books and made her crave more from Tom. She wanted to be ravished by the power of his passion. She ached to be thrown into the spinning vortex of his desire.

But her shy hints to that effect weren't enough, and as the year progressed their relationship remained frustratingly chaste.

Late in her third term, after a student dinner and too many drinks of a punch she'd thought non-alcoholic, a dizzy Poppy found herself climbing through a half-open window into his flat. Tom wasn't home and, half shocked but half delighted by her daring, she undressed and climbed into his bed to wait for him.

He wasn't long. But he wasn't alone either.

Poppy stared dazedly at Adele Jackson, a beautiful nurse who she knew worked on his ward. In the half-light that streamed into the flat from a lamp outside she looked stunning: long, shimmering blonde hair and a glittering tight dress that clung to voluptuously full breasts.

Adele's laugh oozed pure sensuality as she tugged Tom's hand away from the light switch. 'It's nice like this,' she protested. 'Give me another gin. That battle-axe of a sister was watching me like a hawk.'

'Coffee's a better idea.' But Tom was laughing and Poppy froze as he groped for another light switch near the bed. 'Just let me find those notes you wanted—'

Before Poppy could say anything, do anything, move anywhere but from where she sat bolt upright on his bed, the sheet clutched to her small bare breasts, Adele launched herself into Tom's arms and they were kissing—and then he unbalanced and the couple fell onto the bed and directly onto her.

There was her yelp of pain, followed by a flurry of confusion and then a long, ghastly silence.

Of all of them, she realised later, Tom had seemed the least shocked. In fact, there might even have been amusement in the narrowed look that had flickered across her pale, trembling body before they'd disentangled themselves.

Adele, though, was furious. She shouted her rage at both of them then stormed out of the flat.

The slam of the door startled Poppy from fright into mortified shame, and Tom covered her with the sheet again and sat beside her. After a few moments of quiet he'd gently explained that his fondness for her was purely brotherly. 'Concentrate on your studies,' he advised, while she stared at her wringing hands. 'Pass your exams before you start thinking about men.'

But Poppy understood what he was really saying and as he spoke she wept inside, bruised and torn by the awful truth that had hit her like a concrete brick.

She'd made a complete fool of herself. She was just an absurd, flat-chested girl with a brain full of silly fantasies, while a man like Tom could have his choice of beautiful, sexy women. Obviously he'd never viewed her romantically—in fact, if it hadn't been for his friendship with Jeremy he'd never have looked at her twice.

But being rational about it didn't take away the pain. She walked numbly beside him as he escorted her back to the college, then fled up to her room in a flood of wrenching sobs.

Her room-mate and two other students were still up, sharing bottles of wine left from the party. Worried by her distress, they persuaded her to join them. She swallowed one glass. Then another. And then found herself blurting out the sordid details of her humiliation.

The next day the story was all around the college—and the hospital. Poppy prepared herself to become the butt of mocking jokes and laughter but, instead, her fellow students seemed sympathetic—as if she were an innocent victim rather than the cause of the problem.

Later she discovered that the nurse with Tom that night—the one she'd told her friends about—was the wife of the hospital's senior surgeon, that he'd heard about his wife's affair with his registrar and now the marriage was over.

Shortly afterwards, despite passing the second part of his surgical exams, nobody was surprised when Tom left St John's amid rumours that his contract had not been renewed.

Poppy had never been able to rid herself of guilt. Although she couldn't condone his affair with a married woman—was shocked that the man she'd thought she'd known so well could be capable of such deception—if it hadn't been for her stupid fantasies, or even if afterwards she'd kept her mouth shut, the relationship might have ended without him losing his job.

Tortured by embarrassed shame, she'd avoided him for weeks. Then it was too late and he'd left, without her finding the courage to apologise to him. Nobody seemed to know where he'd gone and, wary of painful teasing from Jeremy, who she knew had known of her youthful crush on his friend, she hadn't ever mentioned Tom again. Instead she'd thrown herself into her work, achieving high grades in virtually every subject at medical school.

Six years later she was more confident professionally and socially but she still thought of him. Remembering the foolish girl who'd hidden in his room that night still made her squirm.

The other legacy of those idyllic youthful feelings for Tom was a romantic dreaminess that she knew more earthy women didn't share.

Her hero had proven himself less than perfect but for a short time she'd glimpsed how a perfect love could feel and she knew she could never settle for anything less.

Poppy woke to find herself sprawled on the floor, her legs held uncomfortably high in the air by hands that gripped her ankles like a vice. She blinked, focused and then promptly squeezed her eyes shut.

'Stop pretending, Poppy Brown. I know you're awake.'

She groaned. He was an apparition. If she stayed very still he'd go away.

The apparition swore and the fingers on her ankles tightened. 'I don't have all day,' grated an impatient male voice which was so familiar that it sent shivers along her nerves. 'Get up or I call a porter and send you to Casualty.'

The threat sounded real. Reluctantly she eased one eye open again. He didn't look real— more like the fantasy man she remembered. Tall and powerful with those achingly dark good looks that made her pulse pound. Her head spun and she was dizzy again.

Blue eyes narrowed, cool now and irritated. He let her legs drop to the ground and when they landed with a hearty thud he held out his hand. 'Up.'

If she were about to be savaged by a fierce alien, Poppy decided, it might as well be by one who looked like Tom. She found herself allowing the apparition to haul her to her feet— feet so wobbly that she clutched at his chest for support.

But when her fingers encountered warm, hard flesh she flinched. 'You're real.'

'Of course I'm bloody real.' His mouth twisted as he disengaged her hand, holding her away from him. 'And you're as mad as ever! You look like you've seen a ghost. What's wrong with you, fainting like that?'

'No breakfast.' Her wide green eyes still dazed, she tilted her head up for although she was of average height he towered above her. Six years had done nothing to dull his appeal, she acknowledged. Her memories weren't exaggerated, not exaggerated at all. 'I didn't think. . .'

He muttered something uncomplimentary. 'Of course you didn't think,' he said grimly, and the air between them thickened. 'You rarely do.'

'Tom. . .?' But she was still struggling to make sense of this as she stared up at him in bewildered shock, resisting the urge to pinch herself. He really was here. Here. Real. No fantasy could be this vibrant, this male, this. . .impatient.

Immediately she felt sick. She'd imagined meeting him again, of course—many, many times—but never like this. In her dreams she was always cool and refined, elegant and sophisticated, impressing him with her maturity and sublime professional competence. Impressing him and perhaps. . . She stopped herself but felt her skin shiver as he clicked his tongue, his eyes blue flint now as if he could read her thoughts.

'Well?' he demanded. 'Explain yourself. Missing one meal shouldn't make you faint.'

Drawing herself very straight, she said carefully, 'Postural hypotension.' At his blank look she added, 'It wasn't just missing breakfast— I must have stood up too quickly.' She saw the corners of his mouth tighten and hurried on, registering the white coat, the stethoscope and the bleeper he wore in his top pocket. 'Do. . .do you work here?'

'What do you think?' Abruptly he flicked the side of her cheek. 'Postural hypotension, my foot. Are you pregnant?'

'No!' It came out as a gasp. She blanched even paler, but managed to stop herself blurting out any nonsense about immaculate conceptions. 'No, of course not.'

'Why "of course"?' He peered at her with an intensity that trebled her nervousness. 'You don't look well.'

'I—I'm late for work.'

'You have to eat.' Tom checked his watch. 'And the queues at McDonald's are too long. . .' He looked at the stairs and muttered, 'Up here.'

He marched her up to the first floor and, turning in the opposite way from the still-deserted Green Ward, steered her along an empty corridor to a broad wooden door labelled SENIOR COMMON-ROOM. He nudged her inside and directed her to an armchair. 'Sit.'

Poppy sat stiffly as he inspected the dreary drapes, the unmatched wooden furniture and the array of daily newspapers for the consultants' perusal, her thoughts racing. If Tom was a surgeon here then their paths were destined to cross from time to time, but it was obvious that he thought her a complete twit. And while, admittedly, he'd caught her at a bad moment, considering what had happened, that wasn't so surprising.

And what about what had happened at St John's? If she'd behaved like an idiot now, she'd behaved doubly so back then. She shifted in her seat. After all these years what could she say?

Minutes later the man whose gaze she'd been avoiding passed her two slices of hot toast, thickly spread with butter and strawberry jam, and a steaming cup of tea. 'Eat.'

Welcoming the excuse to delay talking to him, Poppy ate. Hungrily. For, although he made her self-conscious, the day before had been frantically busy and it hadn't just been breakfast she'd missed.

When she finished he frowned at her crumb-free plate. 'More?'

'No, thank you.' She swallowed her tea and straightened in her chair, cleared her throat and met his dark gaze solemnly. St John's was a long time ago now. It was best that she didn't raise the issue. It would only make things worse and, goodness knows, she'd already given him a bad enough impression. She should concentrate on damage limitation.

'I feel much better now,' she said firmly.

'That was exactly what I needed. Now, perhaps you'd be kind enough to direct me to the casualty department? It's my first day and I'm running a little late.'

Raised eyebrows mocked her formality. 'You're three and a half hours late,' he said flatly. 'More than a little.' But despite that and his earlier claim to be busy, he suddenly seemed in no rush and he leaned back in his chair, crossing his arms behind his head—drawing her startled attention to the wide breadth of his chest. 'Your hair's much longer.'

'Yes.' Poppy didn't know what else to say. Nervously she flicked the weight of its thickness behind her.

The movement revealed more of the shrunken emerald jumper she wore, and when his eyes dropped she flushed, resisting the impulse to cross her arms.

'Is this what every well-dressed casualty officer's wearing these days?' he asked sceptically.

Regretting the panic which had made her choose the first clothes that came to hand, Poppy said, 'My work clothes are in the car.' She shifted her cup and saucer to her left thigh and held them there with deliberate casualness, hoping that he hadn't already noticed the small hole she'd torn in the worn fabric of her jeans as she'd rushed to load her cases into the Honda. 'Perhaps I'll go and change——'

'The nurses will sort something out for you.' His eyes narrowed. 'First tell me why you called me an alien.'

Poppy gasped. The china cup and saucer flew from her hands onto the dark carpet. She dropped to the floor and scrabbled around, trying to retrieve them—her neck and face on fire with embarrassment. Alien. She dimly remembered saying something as she fainted. He knew about the aliens.

'Oh, for God's sake, Poppy!' Tom snatched the cup, which her nervous hands had fumbled again, then took the plate and saucer as well, and for the second time that day hauled her to her feet. 'What's wrong with you?'

'I'm overwrought,' she said faintly. It seemed the only possible answer.

He strode away from her and dumped the dishes into a chipped basin. From the set of his back she thought he was very angry but when he turned she saw that he was merely exasperated. 'You were always overwrought,' he said finally. 'Like a trapped fawn, fighting the ravages of a hostile forest. Nothing's changed.'

Poppy sucked in her cheeks, unhappy with that assessment. She'd changed a great deal since he'd last seen her. 'I haven't slept,' she said stiffly. 'I've been on call at Oxford since Saturday morning and last night there was an emergency and I was in Theatre all night and I didn't have time to pack up my flat until this morning and then the car was jammed in and there was an accident on the M40 and it took ages to get through just one junction.'

She knew she was babbling now but it seemed very, very important that she made him understand that the Poppy he'd seen this morning wasn't the normal cool, self-assured, efficient Poppy she'd become. 'And then the M25 was a disaster and anyway I'd gone the wrong way around—'

'Stop!' He held up one hand like a traffic policeman and she shut her mouth obediently, but clearly her explanation hadn't made him forget the thing she wanted him to forget. 'I suppose it's all those books you used to read.'

Poppy crossed her fingers. 'I only read textbooks now.' It was almost true. For the last few years she'd been far too busy with work to read anything like the volume of fiction she'd managed when she was younger, although she still treasured a few minutes each evening before she fell asleep. 'Textbooks and journals.'

But Tom merely lifted his eyes to the ceiling and muttered, 'Why don't I believe that?', proving that he remembered her better than she'd hoped. He checked his watch again and sighed. 'Casualty, I think, before they send out a search party.'

Poppy lifted a shaky hand and nervously smoothed her hair. She gathered up her bag. 'Perhaps you could explain how——'

'I'll take you.' He waved her towards the corridor.

'There's no need——'

'There's every need.' She read his impatience in the tightness of his mouth as he closed the door behind her so quickly that he would have caught her heels if she hadn't darted out at the last moment. 'God knows where you'll end up otherwise.'

Poppy sniffed. 'I'm perfectly capable——'

'That remains to be seen.'

'There weren't any signs,' she protested, trotting after him. 'I was trying to find Casualty but there weren't any signs.'

If it hadn't been for her determination to prove herself mature and self-assured his doubtful grunt would have provoked an argument, but instead she ignored it. 'This place is deserted.' She peered into Green Ward as they hurried past. 'Where is everybody?'

He spared her a brief glance as she bounded behind him down the stairs. 'Probably at

McDonald's. Special offer today. All burgers ninety-nine pence.'

Bewildered, she repeated, 'McDonald's?'

'Later,' he snapped, turning left at the spot where Poppy had earlier fallen at his feet. 'You've just had toast.'

He marched ahead and Poppy trailed behind, confused. She followed him to the far end of the corridor and then through a set of doors marked 'No Entry' into a large open room, divided into cubicles.

At their entrance a plump blonde nurse in a dark blue smock looked up sharply, but her mouth eased into a welcoming smile when she saw Tom.

'Poppy Brown,' he announced. 'Finally.'

'Sorry I'm so late.' Poppy's eyes flicked between him and the nurse. 'I was on call overnight in Oxford.'

'Then you're not late at all.' Smiling, the nurse shook her hand. 'Welcome to the National, Poppy. I'm Lucy Wright, sister here.' She looked at Tom. 'Shall I do the tour?'

'Please.' He gave Poppy's jumper another pained look. 'And drum up something decent for her to wear, will you, Lucy? The trust won't want the public thinking its doctors are destitute.' Not bothering to wait for a reply, he

turned and strode back through the swinging
doors.

The sister seemed startled by that and for a
few seconds she stood, staring at the rocking
doors, but when Poppy stirred she collected herself and said cheerfully, 'Right, Poppy. Let's
get you settled in.'

With Tom gone, Poppy felt a little of the
tension drain out of her shoulders, although
worry about how at home he'd seemed in
Casualty now vied with discomfort at his obvious relief at being rid of her. 'I really am sorry
about being late,' she said distractedly.

'Don't worry. It's the system that's wrong.'
Lucy tucked a few neat strands of her light
bob behind her ear, the small, precise gesture
reminding Poppy of her own dishevelled state.
'How this place can expect you to finish one
job at nine in the morning and start the next an
hour earlier I haven't figured out.' The sister
directed her to the right. 'Let's grab a coffee
while it's quiet.'

When they were settled in Lucy's office, a
tidy room on the opposite side of the department, Poppy said hopefully, 'That doctor—was
that a rare visit to Casualty? Is he. . .one of the
hospital surgeons?'

Lucy laughed. 'Not exactly.' She took a long
sip of coffee. 'Tom Grainger's Acting Casualty

Consultant. And don't worry,' she added, obviously misinterpreting Poppy's pallor, 'he's not an ogre. Admittedly he was a little abrupt about your clothes just now but normally he's very reasonable.'

Poppy's legs were trembling and she tucked them beneath the desk. 'But the consultant who interviewed me?'

'Roger Newcombe's on a nine-month sabbatical,' Lucy explained. 'In Canada. Tom's due to start as trauma consultant here in August. It's a new position and the funding doesn't start till then so, in the meantime, he agreed to stand in for Roger.'

Poppy sucked in her cheeks. Tom was the consultant here. And for the first two weeks of her attachment she was rostered on duty with the consultant.

'Stop fretting.' Lucy's smile was kindly, as if she was used to soothing nervous SHOs. 'He's very approachable. You'll be fine.'

But Poppy doubted that. It was pretty obvious that Tom wasn't thrilled about working with her. With good reason. She drained her coffee. 'I'd better get started,' she said weakly.

'I'll show you around.' The nurse followed Poppy out of the room. 'The department's not as big as we need but it's still easy to get confused in your first few days.'

Lucy first introduced her to the receptionist and clerical staff, and then to the staff nurses on duty. The names blurred as names invariably blurred for Poppy but she got a strong impression of friendly and competent efficiency.

The first area Lucy showed her in detail was the part of Casualty she'd originally walked into. Catering for 'major' or 'stretcher' cases, this was the biggest section of the department with sixteen stretcher bays, each equipped with basic examination equipment.

Tom was back and she saw him carry an ophthalmoscope between patients in two of the bays but, apart from a cursory glance in her direction, he didn't interrupt her tour.

Along the edge of the area were five small rooms. 'Two for paeds, two gynae and one eye and ENT,' Lucy told her.

Poppy glanced into the rooms, noting the specialised equipment in each—including the slit-lamp microscope in the eye room. Apart from a two-week attachment to an eye ward as a student, she'd had little experience of eye injuries and no idea how to use the device.

But once again Lucy proved her experience. 'The eye reg will explain everything this afternoon at your induction,' she said soothingly. 'It won't take long to learn.'

Poppy smiled. 'You've done this job before.'

'Dozens of times.' The sister pushed open a pair of doors, leading off the side of the major area. 'This is Resusc. Either Tom or one of the anaesthetists will go over the equipment for you later.'

Poppy nodded, hoping that it would be an anaesthetist. She looked quickly around the suite, registering the three beds, anaesthetic machines and resuscitation equipment. She noticed another door at the side. 'Another room?'

'Exit to the chopper landing pad.'

Next the sister showed her a small operating theatre, used for minor surgery and suturing, and after that the observation ward, a ten-bedded ward for casualty patients who need to be observed temporarily without full hospital admission. Then she took Poppy to the 'minor' area—six small cubicles and two consulting rooms, separated from the main part by the clerical area and the waiting rooms—designated for people who could be classified as 'walking wounded'.

She met Derek, another newly appointed casualty officer. He told her that Tom had assigned him to deal with patients on the minors side for the morning, and that they would take turns covering it. 'Piece of cake,' he whispered brightly. 'I've only been here a couple of hours and already got it worked out. Examine the patient, request an X-ray and then ask a nurse what to do.'

Poppy smiled as Lucy led her away.

Behind 'minors' was a small X-ray department, plus an orthopaedic suite and plaster room. The sluice, treatment rooms, equipment room and storerooms were at the rear of the department and merited only a cursory inspection. At the far end, near Lucy's office, was a staff tearoom, a big common-room that she'd share with the other casualty officers, another for the two registrars and, beside that, Tom's office.

Lucy directed her back towards the common-room and opened a cupboard door, revealing a rack of white coats in assorted lengths. 'Not exactly flattering,' she said with a wry grimace, 'but at least they keep your clothes clean. Take your pick.'

Poppy frowned at the jumper and jeans that had irritated her new boss so much. The coat might make her look a little more professional but it wouldn't hide what she was wearing. 'It will only take me five minutes to run and change into something better.' Five minutes if she could remember where she'd left the car— longer if she couldn't.

'No need.' The sister pulled open a drawer

to reveal a pile of blue theatre smocks. 'We keep these here for little emergencies.' She laughed at Poppy's puzzlement. 'Bleeding wounds and incontinent babies wreak havoc,' she said lightly. 'Never wear anything here that's dry-clean only—it'll cost you a fortune.'

She gave Poppy's arm a kindly pat, warm eyes twinkling. 'And don't look so nervous,' she chided. 'In two weeks you'll be striding around here like you own the place.'

Poppy smiled her thanks as Lucy left the room. She *was* nervous about her job, she reflected, studying the treatment protocols taped to the wall in the office. But, apart from the worries that stemmed from meeting Tom again, it was only the normal nervousness that came with any new job. Six frantic months of general medicine and six months of a busy surgical job as a house officer had given her a good ground-ing in both fields, and she was confident that she'd mastered the basic skills she'd need as a senior house officer here. And, although it would take time to get used to the peculiarities of casualty work, new equipment and new pro-cedures, she was keen to learn.

Then she saw Tom's signature at the bottom of a memo, outlining the programme for the induction meeting at two, and groaned. Alien! For those few seconds before she fainted she'd genuinely thought he was an alien. Even with the excuse of extreme tiredness, it didn't bear thinking about.

How on earth could she make Tom forget that? He was her boss now. After such a dreadful start what chance did she have of convincing him that the scatty student he'd known was now a mature, capable doctor?

CHAPTER TWO

Lucy smiled brightly at Poppy when she emerged. 'Don't forget you've only an hour and a half before your induction meeting but, in the meantime, there's a six-year-old in room four.' She handed her some notes attached to a clipboard. 'Abdo pain. GP thinks it's appendicitis but didn't bother calling the surgeons.'

She pointed to a white-board on the wall. 'If you need to contact the on-call registrars there are the bleeper numbers. Dial eight-one to bleep then zero before this extension.'

Poppy returned her smile with a thin one of her own and opened the notes, skimming them as she walked towards the room. The child had been seen by one of the nurses who'd noted a history and some observations. He had a slight temperature, 37.8°, mild tachycardia of 104, urinalysis clear.

She opened the door, smiled at the woman she knew from the notes to be the boy's mother, then crouched by his bed. 'Hi. I'm Dr Brown, and you must be Nathan.'

The boy nodded. His face was flushed, although the area around his mouth was pale, and his distress was obvious from the stiff way he was holding himself. 'My tummy hurts.'

Between Nathan and his mother Poppy established that he'd had the pain for about eighteen hours. Initially it had been central but had now localised to the right lower part of his abdomen. He'd been off his food and had been sick once prior to coming into hospital.

'Any recent coughs, colds, sore throats?'

Nathan's mother shook her head. 'Until the pain he's been fine.'

Poppy ran through a routine series of questions, making sure that there was no significant past history or allergies that she needed to know about. Then she examined him, checking his mouth, throat, ears and chest. A virus could cause the lymph glands in a child's abdomen to swell, giving very similar symptoms to appendicitis, and it was important to try and exclude that.

But his top half seemed clear. She lifted his T-shirt. 'Cough for me, Nathan.'

His feeble effort and the way he caught his breath confirmed what she already suspected. She held her hand a few inches above his skin. 'Now blow your tummy out.'

'I can't,' he told her weakly. 'Hurts.'

'OK.' Gently she probed his abdomen, noting the guarding of his muscles in the right lower quadrant and the way he gasped when she removed her hand quickly. That clinched the diagnosis as far as she was concerned. 'Good boy.'

She smiled at his mother. 'Your GP's right. It looks like appendicitis. I'll ask one of the surgeons to come and look, and if he or she agrees it'll mean an operation today.'

'My doctor said he might need an X-ray.'

Poppy shook her head. 'No X-rays,' she said firmly. 'It wouldn't help. I do need to put a tiny needle into his arm,' she admitted, 'but we'll put some magic cream on so it doesn't hurt.'

Nathan's eyes widened. 'Magic cream,' he said in wonder.

'That's right.' She smiled, then looked back at his mother. 'When did he last eat or drink?'

'Water last night, that's all. About nine.'

'Good.' So they could operate at any time now. After explaining that there'd be a short wait, she left them and walked to the bench where all the notes and stationery were stored. She filled out a prescription sheet and handed it to one of the nurses, asking her to apply the EMLA cream immediately. The cream would numb Nathan's skin so that inserting a Venflon would be painless.

She paged the on-call registrar, finishing her notes while she waited for a response and explaining her findings to him when he rang back. 'Looks like appendicitis,' she told him, 'although I haven't an FBC yet as we've only just put the EMLA cream on. He'll need a drip so I thought I'd take the blood out of that.'

'Fine.' He didn't sound worried by the lack of a blood result. 'I'm waiting for my SHO to bring our lunch from McDonald's, then I'll be down.'

Poppy lowered the receiver, wondering at that. McDonald's certainly did a roaring trade if this and the absence of people in Green Ward was anything to go by. Perhaps that sign in the corridor had been warranted after all? She left the notes in the box assigned for surgical referrals and took the next set of notes in the casualty pile.

By the time she'd finished seeing that patient, a thirty-year-old man with a headache that she was confident was migrainous, the surgical registrar had seen her first patient. When she introduced herself he grinned approvingly. 'I agree. He's going straight to the ward. We'll do the drip up there.'

She smiled her thanks and he winked. 'First day?'

Poppy nodded. 'First patient.'

He patted her on the back as he walked past on his way out of the department. 'You'll be all right,' he said, the soothing tone of his voice so similar to Lucy's earlier that Poppy decided she must look like a nervous wreck. 'Your head's screwed on straight.'

Wishing that Tom was so easily convinced, Poppy almost walked into him.

'Run out of work?'

She flushed, meeting his cool stare nervously. 'No. I. . .' Why did she have to sound like such an idiot around him? 'Yes.'

'Bay four.' He pushed another file into her hands. 'Fractured neck of femur.'

She blinked, then looked around vaguely. 'X-rays?'

'Clinical diagnosis.' He picked up another set of notes, eyeing her impatiently now. 'I saw the ambulance crew wheel her in. See what you think.'

'F-fine.' Clutching the notes to her chest, Poppy walked swiftly to the bay and pulled the curtains sharply across behind her. 'Mrs. . . Bartlet,' she said, checking the file to make sure she got the name right, 'I'm Dr Brown.'

The elderly woman managed a smile, although the strain on her face suggested that she was in considerable discomfort. 'I fell down the steps, dear. I've broken my leg.'

Poppy took a brief history and examined her chest and heart, making sure that she wasn't compromised by any blood loss before turning to the hip. Her right leg, the painful one, was a good two inches shorter than the left and externally rotated. There was no obvious sensory loss and her foot pulses were good.

'You're right,' Poppy told her. 'I'm going to put a needle in your arm so I can take blood for testing and give you something for the pain. Then you'll need X-rays. If it is a fracture the orthopaedic doctors will want to operate, probably today.'

Mrs Bartlet nodded weakly. 'Thank you, dear. Just something for the pain.'

Poppy pulled across the IV trolley, applied a tourniquet around her patient's arm, swabbed the skin and inserted a Venflon into a vein on her forearm. She connected a syringe to the cannula and withdrew enough blood to check a blood count, electrolytes and to do a cross-match.

Finally she released the tourniquet, flushed the cannula with saline and taped it firmly in place ready to receive analgesia and intravenous fluids.

When she emerged Tom wasn't around but Lucy was there to show her how to use the computer to order X-rays. She requested urgent views of Mrs Bartlet's hip and pelvis, as well as a chest X-ray. In view of her age and a history of heavy smoking, Poppy knew that the anaesthetist would want to look at the chest X-ray.

She prescribed pain relief and something to stop any nausea, together with intravenous fluids. While Lucy organised them Poppy filled in the forms for the blood she'd taken, handed them to a porter to take to the labs and completed her notes.

While waiting for the X-rays, she saw another patient—a fourteen-year-old girl who'd been brought in by ambulance after having a seizure at school. The fit had been generalised but short and not repeated, and now she was asleep on the trolley. The nurses had checked her BM stix—to make sure her blood sugar was normal—and all other observations were normal.

'She has epilepsy,' explained the girl's mother, 'but she hasn't had a fit for over a year.'

Poppy looked up from where she'd been examining her patient's eyes. 'Still taking valproate?'

'Not always.' The woman looked so anxious that Poppy didn't say anything. 'But I'll make sure she does now.'

'Everything looks fine,' Poppy said once she'd finished examining the girl. Aside from the drowsiness, which was normal after a seizure, there were no abnormalities suggesting any reason for the seizure other than the child's epilepsy. 'I'd like to do a blood test but that's all. If that's all right you can take her home. When are you due to see a specialist again?'

'Next Monday. We go every six months but since it had been so long since the last seizure we'd hoped that he'd stop the medication this time.'

Poppy nodded sympathetically. 'I'm sorry. These things are unpredictable. I'll write you a note to take along and the specialist will be able to check the blood results on the computer.'

By the time she'd written the notes and organised the blood count and liver function tests, Mrs Bartlet's X-rays were back. She located the fracture line exactly where Tom had predicted and bleeped the on-call orthopaedic registrar. 'I cross-matched two units just in case, but her haemoglobin's thirteen at present so she won't need anything pre-op.'

'Great.' The registrar sounded almost enthusiastic. 'We've theatre time this afternoon. When did she last eat or drink?'

'Breakfast at eight.' Poppy checked her watch. It was almost two now so they could operate safely this afternoon. 'We'll do an ECG here to save time.'

'You're an angel. Trying to get an ECG on the ward's like trying to eat concrete. I've just grabbed a spot of lunch but I'll finish my burger and be along to see her in a few minutes.'

Poppy lowered the receiver, frowning. Did everyone eat at McDonald's?

The staff nurse who was looking after Mrs Bartlet was wheeling a sigmoidoscopy kit towards one of the other bays, and Poppy quickly told her that the orthopod was coming and asked about the ECG.

'The technician's on her way.' The nurse smiled. 'You look remarkably in control for your first day.'

Poppy returned her smile gratefully, appreciating the reassurance. 'I think I might even be enjoying myself,' she confessed. Well, work-wise at least.

She checked Mrs Bartlet, restful now that she'd had diamorphine, and explained about her fracture and the need for an operation to fix it. 'They'll either put a plate and pins in,' she told her, 'or else replace the top part of your leg with a prosthesis.' It had been eighteen months since she'd seen any orthopaedics and her memory was hazy, but her patient didn't seem worried.

'I don't mind, Doctor.' Mrs Bartlet gave her a beatific smile and Poppy sucked in her cheeks, counting her patient's respiratory rate in case she was especially sensitive to opiates.

'Anything,' her patient added dreamily. To Poppy's relief, her breathing rate was normal—meaning that the dose wasn't too high. 'Thank you so-o much.'

Making a mental note to check on her again in a few minutes, Poppy selected another file. Returning to the desk a few minutes later, she noticed a blond doctor inspecting Mrs Bartlet's films. 'I'm Poppy Brown,' she said, her eyes on the still-unopened McDonald's apple pie in his pocket. Resisting the temptation to ask how he'd enjoyed his burger, she explained, 'One of the new cas officers. Were we speaking before?'

'Sure were.' He shook her hand, his smile warm and friendly. 'Greg Lund. Ortho SR.' He nodded towards Mrs Bartlet's cubicle. 'Congratulations on the analgesia,' he said easily. 'Exactly right. She's relaxed as anything.'

'What do you think of the films?'

He dragged one finger along the fracture line. 'Nasty.'

'What do you do for a fracture that goes right up like that? A hemiarthroplasty?'

He nodded. 'Safer than trying to pin it.' He tilted his head. 'Keen on orthopaedics?'

'I haven't done any since med school,' she confessed, 'but I like all areas of surgery.' She knew he wouldn't want to hear about everything else that interested her—it was practically every speciality she'd ever studied.

She'd only whittled her final career choice down to surgery after hours of discussion with her brother and father—both surgeons themselves—and she still felt pangs of loss at the thought of giving up medicine and paediatrics, both specialities she'd enjoyed hugely. 'I'd like to get onto the surgical rotation here after this job.'

The registrar nodded. 'It's a good course.' He picked up Mrs Bartlet's file. 'One of the best training schemes in London.'

Poppy knew that: the excellent training was the reason she'd applied to do casualty at the National. She tilted her head, interested in any advice he had to offer about getting a place on the scheme. 'Did you do the course—?'

'Dr Brown!'

They both jumped at Tom's impatient interjection. Poppy whirled around, promptly dropped the notes she was holding then winced at his scowl.

'It's well after two,' he added tightly. 'You're delaying the start of the induction course. I've had to leave the session to come and find you.'

'S-sorry.' Flushing, she crouched to pick up the papers she'd scattered and shoved them all into the brown folder, dimly aware that the orthopaedic SR had melted away. When she'd finally retrieved everything she put the file onto the desk, avoiding looking at him as she nervously flicked her hair back over her shoulders.

'And can't you tie that back?'

Her head snapped up and she lifted a protective hand to her hair. 'I—I usually do,' she stammered. 'But this morning—'

'I know. I know. You were running late.' He leaned forward. 'You're always running late, Poppy Brown. You might have got away with it before but not while you're working for me. I will not let you bring chaos to my department. Understand?'

She nodded mutely, bravely holding his hard gaze. Cool and efficient and self-assured. She had to be cool and efficient and self-assured. But it was so hard when everything kept going wrong.

Tom clapped his hands. 'Hurry along. Your colleagues are waiting for you in the seminar room.'

But she hesitated and as his glare sharpened she said quietly—quietly and coolly and with desperate self-assurance—'I don't know where to go.' She darted a quick look towards the casualty sister, looking at them from one of the cubicles. 'Lucy didn't actually show me where it was.'

'This way,' Tom said tightly. As if she were

a recalcitrant child, he engulfed her small hand in his large warm one and marched her towards the rear doors.

The last thing Poppy saw as the doors swung shut behind them was Lucy's astonished face as she stood watching Poppy being hauled away.

He led her twenty yards down the corridor, not releasing her hand until they stood in front of the door marked 'SEMINAR ROOM'. He opened the door and directed her to a seat, then sat on the desk at the front of the room and—as if nothing untoward had happened—calmly began to outline what he expected of them as casualty officers.

Poppy struggled to concentrate on what he was saying, but all she could think about was the tingling in her hand as it pulsed from where he'd held it. Why did he affect her like this? she wondered with sick bewilderment. Why did she react to him like this after all these years?

After Tom, several registrars took it in turns to discuss how referrals and follow-ups should be handled and to explain what the SHOs would be expected to deal with themselves.

They were followed by representatives from the pathology laboratories, X-Ray, Community Services and Out-patients, who each explained what the new doctors needed to know about their departments.

At the end of the session Poppy's head was reeling with information and the effort she'd had to make to concentrate on what they'd all said.

To her relief the speakers had prepared a booklet, containing summaries of their talks and other facts they needed to know about the hospital, and as the SHOs filed out of the room Tom, propped casually against the edge of the desk with his long legs crossed at the ankles, handed them each a copy.

'Look alive, Dr Brown,' he muttered as he held out hers.

Poppy took the booklet quickly, partially lowering her head both to conceal her flush and to avoid those shrewd, assessing eyes. *Look alive?* Despite having had no sleep in days, she hadn't felt more alive in years!

As Lucy had predicted, one of the eye registrars demonstrated the use of the slit-lamp microscope, showing them how to use the equipment to examine each internal part of the eye and then how to use its magnifying properties to help them locate and remove foreign bodies that could lodge on the cornea.

'You'll see a lot of metal injuries,' she told them, using a plastic model to show them how to lift the fragments, using a sterile needle. 'The vast majority are corneal foreign bodies. There are plenty of local mechanical workshops, particularly to the north of here. On average we see several eye injuries each day.'

She demonstrated how they should use small dye-impregnated strips to flood the eye with fluorescein, which would adhere to any damaged part of the cornea and show up green under the microscope. 'Give the patient analgesia and an eye pad and—if there's any damage—antibiotics as well. They should return two days later and you must check the eye thoroughly.'

She continued by stressing that if they couldn't remove the object, or there was a large rust ring or infection or any suggestion that an object had actually penetrated the eye, then the on-call eye registrar should be contacted immediately. 'There're several good ophthalmology texts in your library for reference,' she said. 'Skip through them and refer to them in more depth if a difficult case comes up.'

Poppy tilted her head, the eye registrar's words bringing home to her the reality of her new job. As a house officer she'd been heavily supervised—that was the nature of the job. It was always someone higher who made the decisions that counted. But here, in Casualty, she had her first opportunity to use her years of training effectively.

She was responsible for her patients here.

There was back-up if she needed it but she had to make decisions. It was a heady thought. Heady. . .and exhilarating.

Then Tom appeared in the doorway behind the registrar. He folded his arms and leaned against the frame, a simple movement, but one he performed with a lazy masculine grace that made her tense.

Unhappily, she found herself noticing the way his posture accentuated the taut, muscled line of his thighs but at that moment, as if sensing her regard, Tom looked directly at her, the sudden tightness of his mouth and the cold way his eyes narrowed telling her that he didn't appreciate the attention.

Poppy looked hastily away and covered her confusion by staring fixedly at the microscope, all the while rubbing her damp palms against her white coat. How was it that her hands could be so moist while her mouth felt uncomfortably parched?

'Any problems, ask for help,' the registrar was saying. 'One of us is always on call.' She turned slightly, saw Tom, then smiled prettily, losing her businesslike briskness. 'All yours,' she said, her voice promptly dropping an octave.

The only other girl among the casualty officers was standing next to Poppy, and at that she nudged her then rolled her eyes expressively and mimed sticking a finger down her throat. While Poppy smiled Tom clearly hadn't found anything unusual in the registrar's behaviour.

He merely murmured an impersonal, 'Thanks,' then straightened, indicating with his head that the group should follow him. Seven new casualty officers trotted after him, Poppy dragging her feet at the rear.

He took them to Resusc and they gathered around a bed, Poppy taking care to stand furthermost away from Tom as he outlined the resuscitation equipment. 'Before the arrival of more senior staff your job is to begin resuscitation,' he said. He demonstrated the use of the defibrillator, showed them the cabinet where the emergency drugs were stored and opened the drawer containing the anaesthetic equipment.

'In an ideal world intubation is an anaesthetist's job,' he said, 'but conditions are not always ideal. Accordingly, I've arranged for each of you to spend one half-day attached to an anaesthetist in main theatres to improve your skills, starting this week.'

There was a general murmur of appreciation at that, a feeling which Poppy shared. As a student she'd been taught how to place the anaesthetic tube directly into a patient's trachea,

but it was a specialised skill that needed practice
and she welcomed the opportunity.

Next, Tom ran through the standard resuscitation procedure, a protocol with which she was
fully conversant after her time in general
medicine.

He strode to the large cupboards that formed
the far wall of the room and, like sheep, they
followed him. 'You'll find most of the equipment you'll need here.' He slid open the doors
to reveal shelves of packages. 'Suture sets, chest
drain sets, central-line kits, splints, pacing
equipment. . .' His hands slid the length of the
cupboard. 'Look through it as soon as you get
a chance and familiarise yourself with what's
available and how to use it.'

Poppy lifted herself up on tiptoe, studying
the supplies—deducing from the renewed alert-
ness of the other SHOs that they, too, were
excited about the emergency side of their new
job.

The last cupboard contained assorted intravenous fluids and a fridge. 'O negative blood,'
Tom told them. 'Avoid using unless you have
to but remember it saves lives. For those of you
on nights we've rostered one of our casualty
registrars on with you tonight and she'll take
you over our trauma procedures and your role

on the trauma team, but the rest of you will learn about that tomorrow.'

A quick glance at her watch told Poppy why they couldn't learn now. It was already after six. The afternoon had flown past.

'Finally, today. . .' Tom directed them to the small machine beside the last bed '. . .this is a simple Coulter counter.' He inserted a form into the printer beside the machine then loosened the purple top of a tube of blood and held it up to the needle that protruded out of the machine, pressing a button labelled 'sample'.

'It takes a few seconds to get a haemoglobin, white count and platelets.' When a green light flashed he withdrew the tube and wiped the needle. Soon afterwards the printer became activated, producing a neatly filled-in summary of the results. 'Leave the sample here,' he said, indicating the rack on top of the machine. 'Haematology will check results to monitor accuracy.'

He turned to the basin and soaped his hands, continuing to address them although he was facing away. Poppy found herself watching the strong line of his broad back beneath his white coat and the way his short, dark hair was just beginning to curl at the ends into his neck.

'We've only had the machine a few months,' he was saying as he swivelled back to them, forcing Poppy to avert her eyes hurriedly again, 'and we have it on trial on resusc patients at present. It saves time and if we can get the funding we want to buy it to use for all our patients here.'

'What about electrolytes?' asked the doctor who was sharing her casualty shift. 'Any chance of a machine to check those?'

'Afraid not.' Tom shook his head regretfully. 'At least not yet. Money's tight.'

'How about a microscope?' The pretty SHO who'd nudged Poppy earlier looked enthusiastic. 'So we can check urines ourselves.'

'One step at a time. It's taken two months of campaigning to get this installed.' He smiled at her apparent dismay. 'Let me guess. A budding microbiologist?'

The doctor grimaced. 'Microbiologist or physician,' she confirmed. 'Hopefully, this job will sort out which.'

'This job might change the plans of every one of you.' He surveyed the whole group and, although she kept her eyes fixed on the sober pattern of his tie, Poppy felt his gaze linger fractionally on her stiff face. 'It's demanding and stressful, but if you keep your minds on your jobs and work hard and concentrate on doing your best, rather than just getting by, you'll learn a great deal. About yourselves as well as about medicine.'

Just as Poppy looked up he clapped his hands, breaking the suddenly serious mood with a lazy grin that set her pulse racing again. 'Right, ladies and gentlemen. End of speeches. See you tomorrow. Two o'clock.'

As the group began to disperse he turned his attention pointedly to Poppy, and for the umpteenth time she felt her face fill with colour. 'Eight o'clock sharp tomorrow for you,' he added, more softly. 'Think you can manage that, Dr Brown?'

'I—I won't be late,' she said stiffly.

'I'll believe that when I see it,' he said flatly.

Poppy followed the rest of the SHOs along the corridor towards the common-room.

'God, he's exciting!' The blonde girl who'd asked him about the microscope gave Poppy a bemused smile. 'Don't you think?'

Poppy shrugged weakly, not needing to ask who she was referring to. 'He's OK.'

The girl rolled beautiful grey eyes. 'OK?' she squealed. 'He's magnetic! I'm still trembling. When he turned that smile on me my legs melted.' She held out her hand. 'Hi! Kim Farrelly. And you must be gay.'

'Poppy Brown. And, no, I'm not.' But Kim had an infectious smile and, despite her shock at the question, Poppy found herself smiling back. 'Are you normally so direct?'

'Mostly.' They were alone in the corridor alongside Casualty now, the other SHOs having wandered into the common-room. 'At least admit he's gorgeous.'

But Poppy wasn't going to admit anything. 'I'm here to work,' she said lightly.

'Then he's all mine.' She pulled a mocking face. 'Well, mine and that ridiculously serious eye reg's.' Then she laughed. 'In my dreams, at least.'

Poppy's head jerked. 'He's not married, then?'

'Too much of a workaholic.' Kim grinned. 'Unbelievable, isn't it? Gorgeous, powerful *and* single. He's back in Britain now with a good consultant position lined up. My guess is that the next step's a wife.' She fluttered her eyelashes. 'And I'm available.'

Poppy laughed; she couldn't help it—the girl was outrageous. But one thing stuck in her mind. 'You said, "back in Britain". Has he been away?'

'More than five years in the States,' the blonde girl confirmed. She leaned forward and peered along the corridor, as if checking that it was clear. 'There was a bit of a scandal,' she hissed. 'Apparently, when he was a registrar at

St John's he had a fling with a married nurse. The husband turned out to be some bigwig in the College of Surgeons and when he found out Tom lost his job. He ended up leaving the country to let the dust settle!'

Poppy paled. Tom had left Britain? No wonder she'd heard no mention of him over the years. Hoarsely she demanded, 'How do you know all this?'

'You know what hospitals are like.' Kim's shrug was philosophical. 'I've been doing my surgical job here the last six months.'

Abruptly, Poppy straightened, horribly fascinated but guiltily aware that she was gossiping. 'Er. . .what shift are you doing?'

'Start with shift five,' the blonde girl answered as they started walking towards the common-room again. 'Long days at the weekend. Nights next week. You?'

'Number two,' she said. 'Weekdays.'

Kim's warm, dancing eyes suggested she was aware that that meant working with Tom. 'Lucky girl.'

Poppy made a noncommittal sound, glad that they'd reached the common-room so that she didn't have to think of another answer. She smiled a distracted greeting at the other doctors, who were lounging around the room chatting, and let Kim introduce her again.

'Poppy?' A tall, thin, studious-looking SHO, who she thought might be called Paul, looked at her with twinkling brown eyes. 'After your hair?'

'After my mother's garden,' she told him, lifting self-conscious hands to flick her hair behind her back. 'I'm a May baby.'

'I like it,' said Kim. 'It suits you. It's. . .exotic.'

Poppy grimaced. Red hair and freckles didn't seem particularly exotic to her, but there was no need to reply because a sudden heavy thudding outside distracted the others and sent them hurrying to the window.

Curious, she followed. The helicopter was easy to spot, with its distinctive orange markings. It was low, and heading directly towards the hospital. As it neared the thudding was replaced by a high-pitched whirring sound. Poppy's eyes dropped to the car park beneath the window and her breath caught with shock.

It was obvious where the chopper planned to land. Obvious because the area was surrounded by a large red circle painted on the ground with 'Strictly No Parking' painted across the centre.

A circle of concrete that was empty apart from one small dented Honda Civic, parked jauntily inside the rim. *Poppy's* Honda Civic.

CHAPTER THREE

POPPY tore out of the room and along the corridor. Remembering the door Lucy had shown her earlier, she hurried into Resusc.

The room was crowded, the trauma team's doctors and nurses busy with the equipment—obviously preparing for the casualty. The door to the landing pad was open, manned by orderlies in blue coats holding two stretchers, and she headed straight for it—slipping between them to reach the exit.

'What the hell is that bloody car doing there?'

Poppy glanced at Tom when he suddenly appeared beside her, noting his tight anger and flinching from the harshness of his voice. He was glaring at the Honda, not at her, and—stiff with misery and embarrassment—she stayed quiet.

It was too late to move the car as the helicopter was already landing. It manoeuvred itself to the far side of the circle away from the vehicle, the noise of its engine screaming from so close and the draught sweeping her hair upward into a frantic spiral that flicked towards Tom. Grabbing great handfuls of the stuff, she clutched the errant strands against her head and tried to hold them down.

He glanced briefly in her direction, saw the difficulty she was having and twisted his mouth derisively as if to emphasise how impractical he thought it. Then the chopper was down and he was running half-crouched towards it, quickly followed by the orderlies.

Poppy watched them unload one patient, a doctor who'd been on board the helicopter continuing to bag the patient while a nurse did regular cardiac compressions as the trolley was wheeled past her into Resusc. There were too many other doctors and nurses around the bed already for Poppy to get any more than a brief glimpse of an unconscious middle-aged man.

Another trolley raced out and Tom helped to unload a second patient—a young man, who was conscious but encased in one of the bulky MAST suits designed to help casualties maintain their blood pressure—suggesting that the emergency crew suspected internal injuries and bleeding.

Tom kept one hand on the man's carotid pulse as they wheeled him towards Resusc. 'Ever seen a paracentesis?' he shouted, the noise of the helicopter so loud that she could only just hear him.

'Never.' Poppy raced beside him.

'We'll be doing one here.' Once they were inside he spoke quietly, his voice calm and controlled as he helped shift their patient onto the casualty trolley. 'They were working in a road ditch that collapsed. Likely crush injuries.'

Lucy bent over the boy with her mouth at his ear, explaining everything that was happening and reassuring him, while the other members of the team concentrated on their tasks—each seeming to know automatically what to do.

Things moved very fast. Tom worked with another doctor who Poppy assumed to be another surgeon, swiftly examining the casualty—beginning with his neck and working systematically across his back, chest, abdomen and limbs. When they'd finished, the other surgeon examined their patient's eyes, while Tom instilled some anaesthetic into the side of his neck, followed by a wide-bore intravenous line into his jugular vein.

While all this was going on the nurses were connecting him to monitoring equipment, making preparations for X-rays and hooking up bags of blood to the line Tom had introduced as well as to two peripheral lines which Poppy assumed the helicopter staff had inserted.

Staff around the other man on the opposite side of the room were equally busy but, despite the number of people in the room and the speed with which each was working, far from seeming chaotic the room hummed with organised efficiency.

Tom pulled on another pair of gloves, nodding for Poppy to do the same, then with one foot he hauled a prepared trolley between them. While she swabbed the central area of the man's abdomen indicated by Tom, he prepared the equipment. Lucy quietly explained to the patient what he was doing as he instilled some anaesthetic, made a tiny stab with the scalpel and inserted a long cannula into the abdominal cavity.

Understanding what was required, Poppy promptly connected the tubing to a clear plastic bag and let it drop onto the trolley.

Frank blood poured into the bag, confirming that there were internal injuries. 'Theatre one,' Tom commanded. 'Stat.' He lifted his head towards the other surgeon. 'Want a hand?'

As casualty consultant he wouldn't normally be involved in operating on patients, but the other man's immediate acceptance of the offer reminded Poppy that Tom's background was in trauma surgery. Clearly, even though officially working in Casualty at present, his operating skills weren't being wasted.

Poppy helped to steer the trolley towards the

lift at the end of the room—a lift which led directly to the emergency theatre suite—but as several other members of the surgical team had now arrived she didn't need to join them for the ride up.

Tom in the meantime, was checking the progress of the other casualty. 'Bilateral chest drains, second intercostal space,' she heard him say before the scream of the helicopter muffled the rest of his words.

The noise of the chopper taking off reminded her about her car, and she hurried outside and moved the forlorn-looking Honda into a legal space. Tom wasn't in Resusc when she got back so she assumed that he'd gone up to Theatre. The casualty officers were still busy trying to resuscitate the other patient from the helicopter. Although it was well after seven, and she should have been off duty at six, Poppy worried that minors was not being covered so she went to check.

Predictably, it was crowded. The staff nurse working there assured her that there weren't any emergencies that couldn't wait until one of the on-duty doctors was free and urged her to go home while she had the chance, but it looked so busy that Poppy elected to stay and help.

'Welcome to the madhouse, then.' She

handed Poppy a clipboard. 'Sprained ankle, I think. Cubicle four.'

It took several hours to clear the backlog of patients, and by that time the influx had slowed to a trickle. In a gap while the patients she'd just seen were still waiting for X-rays a weary-looking Lucy brought Poppy and the staff nurse coffee.

Poppy asked her about the earlier emergencies.

Lucy sighed. 'They couldn't get the older man back—massive chest and abdo injures apparently. Tom's still in Theatre with the young one—ruptured spleen, as well as renal and liver tears. Sounds touch and go.'

Both of them were silent for a few minutes, then Poppy said, 'Is it normal for Tom to go to Theatre like that? I mean, even while he's working here in Casualty?'

'He's the best,' said Lucy simply. She took a few sips of coffee. 'You won't believe it but some idiot parked on the chopper landing pad today. The traffic control crews have been so busy policing the queues at McDonald's that they didn't even notice.'

'B-but the helicopter managed to land.'

'The only reason there was no delay was that there just happened to be space the other side.' Lucy sighed. 'Honestly, it's a great red circle and there are signs everywhere. Some people just don't think about the consequences of their actions. I'd like to find the man who owns that car and give him a piece of my mind.'

Poppy flushed. 'I-it's my car.' She saw the sister's mouth drop open but rushed on before she could say anything. 'I was running so late that I didn't even notice where I was parking.'

Lucy's mouth snapped closed. 'Well, it turned out all right,' she said kindly after a few seconds of silence. 'It's obviously possible to miss the signs. It is only your first day.' She took a hurried mouthful of her drink. 'It should be roped off,' she said firmly. 'I'll suggest we rope it off.'

'Thanks.' Poppy smiled weakly, but inwardly she continued to berate herself for her thoughtlessness.

She heard footsteps and saw Tom was at the doorway. 'Still here, Poppy Brown?' He managed a half-smile but there were lines of strain around his eyes. 'This is duty above and beyond.'

Poppy's pulse thumped at his approval although she knew that it would soon dissolve.

Perhaps trying to ward off the confession she suspected was coming, Lucy said quickly, 'Poppy's done a terrific job. Cubicles were overflowing an hour ago.'

'Really?' His brows lifted and his eyes held hers fractionally.

But before he could say anything more Poppy blurted, 'Tom, it was mine. The car in the landing area tonight. I'm sorry.'

Immediately the temperature in the tiny room plunged. 'I should have guessed,' he muttered darkly. 'Of all the—' But then he stopped abruptly as he perhaps saw her misery and realised that she understood exactly how irresponsible she'd been. 'Hell!' He slammed his palm against the doorframe. 'The minute I saw you this morning I knew you'd be trouble.'

Poppy blanched. 'Tom, it was a genuine mistake—'

'Another mistake like that and you're out of a job,' he grated. 'Permanently. Understand?'

She lowered her head. 'Yes.'

'I want order,' he said. 'Order and calm in this department. Is that clear?'

'Yes, Tom.'

'No crises, no *aliens*—' he sounded disgusted '—no hysterical faints and, most of all, no disasters!'

'No, Tom.' She couldn't look up but sat, staring at the floor, until she heard the door slam.

Lucy touched her arm softly, her face pale and shocked. 'That was unfair,' she said, her quiet voice strained. 'I'm sorry.' She darted a quick worried look in the direction of the door. 'I've never seen him so. . .severe.'

'He had good reason.' Poppy managed a weak smile. 'I'd better leave before he comes back.'

Quietly—obviously still struggling to understand Tom's attitude—Lucy said, 'Perhaps. . . perhaps he just lost the young chap in Theatre.'

'Let's hope not.' Poppy made for the door. 'See you tomorrow.'

'Get a good night's sleep. Everything will be fine tomorrow,' said Lucy.

But Poppy didn't believe it.

The next morning she went straight to the common-room where she'd left her coat and equipment the night before. Derek, her casualty officer partner, was already there, sitting at one of the desks taking notes from a textbook. He gave her a strange look as she shrugged out of her jacket, but if he was surprised by her transformation from dishevelled urchin to prim school-marm he didn't comment.

Poppy smoothed her tweed suit and pulled on her white coat, concentrating on pinning her name badge to the lapel. She hoped that the trembling of her fingers wasn't as noticeable to him as it was to her.

Her task completed without pricking herself, she lifted a self-conscious hand to smooth the braid she'd curled tightly into the back of her neck. 'All set?' she said, trying to keep her voice bright without letting the strain show.

He checked his watch, then turned over a page of his book. 'Another fifteen minutes,' he said easily. 'No point in beginning early—they'll start expecting it.'

'I—I think I'd better—since I was so late yesterday.'

Derek shrugged. 'Whatever.' He turned another page. 'I'll be along at eight.'

In the privacy of the corridor Poppy took three deep breaths. 'Calm and self-assured,' she repeated quietly. She would look and behave as a perfect casualty officer. She would be beyond criticism. She would be the most efficient junior doctor Tom had ever worked with. She would be an intellectual.

He was leaning against one of the benches with his long legs crossed in front of him, chatting with the two casualty officers who were about to finish their night shifts. His eyes locked with hers the instant she walked into majors.

Poppy froze, her courage faltering as she acknowledged the nervous way her breath quickened and her palms moistened. After yesterday it was fright, of course—that and the legacy of knowing that her behaviour at St John's had driven him to America—but she would deal with this. She was an adult now, not a silly naïve girl. She clenched her fists. She'd been very tired—overtired yesterday and. . .distraught. Today she would handle this with aplomb.

As she walked stiffly towards them, her new shoes still rigid, the two cas officers smiled a welcome while Tom's eyes narrowed, his gaze faintly incredulous as it lingered on her suit.

'Good morning.' She directed her gaze to her two colleagues. 'Busy night?'

'So-so.' The tall one called Paul grimaced. 'We thought it would be a nightmare—there was a brawl at one of the local pubs and around midnight the place was full of bleeding drunks—but after that it settled.' He grinned at the man by his side. 'Tom tells us that fights are common there.'

'Oh, dear,' she murmured. She lifted her face to Tom himself, straightening defensively at the mockery she sensed in his perusal of her new outfit. 'Any patients for me to see yet?'

He looked deliberately at his watch, the mock-surprised way his eyebrow lifted when he looked back at her prickling her skin like a nettle. 'Not here,' he said finally. 'You'll be covering minors until the second induction meeting.' He paused. 'At two. Sharp.'

When she turned away towards minors, her face burning, he spoke to the others. 'As we now have Dr Brown's able assistance far earlier than any of us could have anticipated,' he said, the sarcasm in his voice subtle but enough to make Poppy falter as she walked awkwardly towards the door, 'you two can head home to bed.'

By mid-morning Poppy was less nervous. She hadn't seen Tom so she assumed he must be fully occupied on the majors side. The nurses were friendly and helpful, and although she'd been expecting some comment about the stupid way she'd parked her car the day before nobody had said anything.

And so far the stream of cuts, scalds, sprained ligaments and broken collar-bones hadn't included anything she couldn't deal with confidently.

Then she saw a sixty-year-old woman, Mrs Agnes Worth, who'd fallen onto her outstretched hand. X-rays confirmed what Poppy had already suspected from the painful deformity of her wrist—a classic Colles' fracture, or fracture of the lower ends of her arm-bones.

Lucy joined her as she studied the films. 'You'll have to reduce that,' she told Poppy with an assurance that suggested long experience. 'There's too much angulation just to plaster it. Have you had a lot of experience with orthopaedics?'

Poppy shook her head. 'As a student, of course, but we didn't do a lot of practical work. One of the registrars is going to go over reductions this afternoon.'

'I'll ask Tom to show you,' the sister said, ignoring Poppy's sharp intake of breath. 'When did she last eat or drink?'

'Last night.'

Lucy smiled. 'Take her through to the plaster room and one of the nurses will help you set up. I'll send him across.' She squeezed Poppy's arm gently. 'Relax! You're doing a superb job. This is quite straightforward.'

But it wasn't the fracture Poppy was worried about. 'I—I could call the ortho reg or SHO,' she said quickly, 'rather than bother Tom.'

'He won't mind,' Lucy answered with a dismissive wave of her hand, but then her smile stilled. 'Forget about how he was last night,' she said more quietly. 'He wouldn't have meant it personally. He enjoys teaching.'

But that didn't mean that he'd enjoy teaching *her*. Poppy helped her patient climb onto the trolley in the plaster room. Nor did it mean that she wouldn't make an idiot of herself by fumbling around as she kept doing when he was close.

The staff nurse laid out the plaster strips they'd need and filled a metal bucket with water. 'We normally use a Bier's block to anaesthetise the arm,' she told Poppy, 'unless there's any specific contraindication.'

Poppy nodded. She'd seen the technique used, and after she'd made sure there was no past history of heart disease, seizures or allergy she explained to Mrs Worth what they'd be doing and witnessed her signature on a consent form.

Tom arrived as she was inserting a Venflon into her patient's left arm, having already installed a butterfly needle into the injured hand for the anaesthetic. To her relief, although she felt herself tense at his presence, her normal skill didn't falter and the cannula slid painlessly into the vein she'd chosen.

As she was flushing the Venflon with saline Derek arrived. Tom introduced himself and the other casualty officer to Mrs Worth, took a short history, examined her arm and finally checked the X-ray.

'Dr Brown. . .' Tom's cool cobalt gaze flickered to her '. . .you'll be responsible for the manipulation. Derek, you'll assist me with the anaesthetic.' He pulled a plastic-encased protocol out of the plaster trolley at the end of the bed and showed them the chart listing the recommended doses of anaesthetic according to the weight of their patient.

He lifted his head. 'How heavy, Carol?'

'Sixty.' The staff nurse pressed three adhesive leads onto Mrs Worth's chest to connect her to an ECG monitor.

Tom traced one finger down the chart. 'Sixty kilos, that's one-eighty milligrams of point five per cent prilocaine, that's thirty-six millilitres.' He handed Derek a vial of the anaesthetic. 'Draw that up.'

'Blood pressure one-thirty over eighty-five,' said Carol, confirming the reading with the digital read-out on the monitor—having already connected the blood pressure cuff to the non-injured arm. 'I've checked both arms.'

'Good.' Tom checked the cuff attached to the trolley, wrapped it around their patient's injured arm—after covering the area with cotton wool—then lifted the arm into the air, passing it to Carol to hold it there while he explained to Mrs Worth what they were about to do.

While they waited for some of the blood to drain out of the arm Tom turned to Poppy again. 'Signs of anaesthetic toxicity?'

She swallowed, momentarily distracted by his eyes. This morning they seemed extraordinarily vivid, not simply cobalt, she realised, but a cobalt-azure blend. The eyes narrowed fractionally and she paled. 'Perioral tingling, restlessness, loss of consciousness,' she said huskily, keeping her voice as low as his to avoid alarming their patient. 'Proceeding to seizures, bradycardia and hypotension, although this drug has relatively low toxicity and serious complications are extremely rare.'

His expression didn't change. 'Treatment?'

'Oxygen. Diazepam for seizures. Treatment for bradycardia and other arrhythmias as appropriate.'

'Minimum time cuff must be inflated?'

She faltered and immediately his attention shifted to her colleague. 'Derek?'

'Twenty minutes,' Derek said confidently, 'ensuring that the drug is completely tissue-bound. If the check X-ray is OK let it down and then re-inflate immediately for two minutes, watching for symptoms.'

'Good.' Then, at Tom's quiet instruction, Derek inflated the cuff up to well above the systolic blood pressure, checked that the radial pulse had disappeared, slowly injected the anaesthetic into the butterfly Poppy had inserted and removed the needle.

While they waited for the anaesthetic to take effect Tom demonstrated the reduction technique on Derek's forearm, and had Poppy imitate the movements to be sure she understood what was required. 'Look at the X-ray,' he told her. 'You're trying to correct the angulation first and then plaster in ulna deviation to oppose the radial displacement.'

She kept her eyes fixed on the X-ray, worried that those eyes would fluster her if she looked up at him again. 'I've never plastered before.'

'I'll demonstrate.'

Mrs Worth's arm was numb now and she looked quite content so obviously the pain was gone. 'Ready at this end,' she said cheerfully.

Tom smiled. He took hold of Mrs Worth's arm above the elbow and said to Poppy, 'Pull now.'

Poppy shot another quick look at the X-ray then took hold of their patient's thumb and fingers and pulled, leaning back to put more weight into the movement—surprised at how much force she needed before she felt the shift that suggested the fragments had disimpacted. Smoothly changed her grip and watching the X-ray again, she carefully manipulated the bones back into what felt like the correct shape.

Carol immediately took Tom's position— gripping Mrs Worth's upper arm—leaving him free to plaster. He dunked the prepared plaster bandages into the bucket and held them beneath the water for a few seconds. The lack of space beside the bench forced him so close to Poppy that even though she held her body rigidly away she could feel the faintly spice-scented heat of him beside her.

He wrung out the plaster and while Poppy held her breath he positioned the slab across the side of the arm, moulded it around the thumb and folded it so that it stopped short of the elbow, before covering it with gauze. Inevitably, as she held Mrs Worth's hand in the correct position, his hands brushed hers and she flinched.

'Now mould the plaster,' he said, his voice low and deep and coming from somewhere beside her left ear. He held Mrs Worth's fingers so that she could release her grip.

Mutely she obeyed his instructions, registering the warmth of the stiffening plaster— although that was mild, compared to the warmth of her face. 'Towards the ulna side,' he added quietly as the plaster solidified. 'That's enough.'

When he moved away to check on Derek Poppy released her breath, sucking mouthfuls of air into her lungs to refill them. She held grimly onto her patient's arm, wanting to wait until the plaster had hardened a little more before trusting it to rest on a pillow. 'All right, Mrs Worth?'

'Fine, dear. Am I cured?'

'Mended, I hope.' Poppy managed a tense smile. 'Carol's asking the radiographer to come back and take another X-ray. If it looks OK we'll take that cuff off your arm and that's the end of it.'

'Will I go home then?'

She dared a quick look at Tom, unsure what the department's protocol was, and although he'd been busy instructing Derek he'd obviously been listening to her as well because he spoke without prompting. 'Two hours' observation first,' he said smoothly. 'And back to fracture clinic tomorrow for a check-up.'

'Tomorrow!' Mrs Worth looked impressed. 'That is good service.'

'We aim to please.' Tom stood out of the way to let the radiographer in to position her machine. When she was ready to take the X-ray Poppy and Derek left the room while Tom stayed, sheltering behind a lead shield and checking that the arm cuff stayed inflated to prevent the anaesthetic escaping.

When the radiographer returned with the check film they studied the picture. The deformity had been corrected and Tom said, 'Good.

Well done,' before telling Derek to release the cuff.

Poppy walked back to the bench and her notes as if she were walking on a cloud. 'Idiot,' she told herself under her breath, but that didn't help her feel any less ridiculously pleased at his praise.

But when she caught herself sneaking glances at him while he helped Derek tidy the anaesthetic trolley on the opposite side of the room she stilled, her pleasure faltering. She remembered those tingling moments when she'd stood so close to him and the way her hand had ached after his touch yesterday, and she frowned.

It was the past, of course. Six years ago the adolescent she'd been had thought herself madly in love with him. However embarrassing that seemed to her now, it wasn't surprising that she was having difficulty reacting to him on a purely professional level—something she'd have to achieve now that he was her consultant if her work wasn't to suffer.

She looked fixedly at her notes. The thing that was making her most self-conscious—and him most irritable—she was sure, was that they'd never resolved what had happened six years ago. She needed to voice her guilt and now had no excuse not to do what she should have done immediately. She would force herself to talk to him about what had happened, she decided, her fists clenching so hard that her nails dug into her palms. After all, she'd almost ruined his career. She had to apologise.

That afternoon, determined not to be late again for the teaching session, Poppy turned down Lucy's invitation to join her at McDonald's and skipped her lunch-break, arriving at the seminar room fifteen minutes before the final part of their induction was scheduled to begin.

Kim, the only person in the room, was sprawled casually in a chair with her long, shapely legs propped on the seat in front, happily munching her way through a Big Mac. Her eyes widened when Poppy walked in. 'God!' she said starkly, swinging her legs to the floor and letting the remains of her hamburger slide back into its box. 'Talk about changing your image. What on earth are you wearing?'

Poppy flushed, sensing that the comment was not meant to be flattering. 'It's new,' she mumbled, sitting down quickly.

Her colleague's astonished gaze dropped to her sensible brogues. 'And those shoes?'

Poppy tucked the offending items under her chair. 'They're very comfortable.'

'And you've cut your hair.'

'Just fastened it back,' she said tautly. 'Are we just doing trauma and orthopaedics this afternoon?'

But Kim clearly wasn't going to be so easily diverted. 'I don't believe it,' she said in wonder. 'Yesterday I had you pegged as some sort of earth-child—all flowing ringlets, white skin and big green eyes—but today you look like my grandmother.'

Poppy averted her eyes. 'Thanks a lot.'

Kim laughed. She tweaked Poppy's tweed jacket. 'This isn't the real Poppy Brown, surely?'

Poppy said firmly, 'It's the new Poppy Brown.' The cool, self-assured Poppy Brown who had been absent yesterday. From now on it was out with the casual shirts and flowing dresses which had formed the bulk of her work attire in the past and in with tailoring and tights. She cleared her throat. 'Good lunch?'

There was a short pause, during which Kim must have decided to let the subject of Poppy's transformation drop for she retrieved her burger again and nodded. 'Long queues, though.' She took another mouthful. 'Practically a whole paediatric ward pushed in front of me.' She munched thoughtfully for a few seconds. 'Would have looked a bit mean—a doctor bawling out all those little kids in wheelchairs—but I tell you I was tempted.'

Poppy gave her a sideways look. 'What is it with McDonald's and this place?' At Kim's puzzled frown she added, 'I mean, surely it isn't normal for all the patients to eat there? What's wrong with hospital food?'

Kim blinked. 'Have you tried the hospital food here?'

Although Poppy was staying in one of the hospital flats until she had a chance to look for somewhere better to live, she'd dialled out for pizza the night before. 'Not yet.'

The spikes of her colleague's silky fringe jumped around as she nodded. 'When you do you'll understand.'

Poppy promptly vowed to avoid it—a decision reinforced by the arrival of several more of her colleagues, all clutching bulging McDonald's paper bags and muttering veiled threats about pushy paediatric patients who jumped queues.

Even Tom, when he arrived—several minutes late, she noted—finished his own burger, before beginning the lecture.

It was probably interesting—nobody appeared bored and Kim beside her looked riveted—but once Poppy saw the sheaf of papers that suggested he'd prepared notes on his talk her attention wandered, and despite her

best efforts to concentrate she found herself nervously rehearsing the apology she planned to
deliver before she left work that night.

She'd be calm, reasoned and rational, she
decided, wondering if his hair felt as soft and
shiny as it looked. She'd combine sincere regret
with a mature air of responsibility, she vowed,
firmly directing her gaze away from the easy
movements of his chiselled mouth as he talked.

Tom, for his part, she decided, studying the
relaxed way he shifted his hands to emphasise
a point, would dismiss the whole episode as
unfortunate but forgotten.

And then everything would be back to normal
and this. . .tension would be gone and she'd be
able to concentrate properly on her work.

It was warm in the room and now he removed
his white coat in a single fluid movement and
slung it across the desk behind him. Half-
impatiently, he rolled up the pale sleeves of his
shirt to reveal strong, hair-roughened wrists and
forearms.

Still talking—the smooth deep flow of his
voice washing over her like warm velvet—he
strode to the white-board at the front of the
room and listed a series of points under a heading 'Multi Trauma'—points used for grading
the severity of the overall injury in a patient
with that diagnosis.

Poppy moistened lips that were suddenly very dry. When he lifted and stretched to complete the chart the fabric of his shirt and dark trousers pulled taut, outlining the muscles beneath, and she took a quick breath.

When he turned back to them he leaned against the desk again, feet crossed at the ankles. Poppy studied his shoes: casual, dark leather boat-style shoes that she liked very much. Her eyes drifted upwards. He had nice legs, she decided, very nice legs. Until yesterday she'd forgotten how nice. Long, muscled, and. . .fantastic thighs. Broad, powerful, altogether quite the best thighs she'd ever seen. The sort of thighs that won competitions, she acknowledged. The sort of thighs that probably turned women's legs weak.

She shifted in her chair and crossed her legs, nervously skipping the next bit of his anatomy.

Good, tight abdomen, she saw, not thin, but pleasantly solid—perfect. Wonderful chest, but, then, she'd known that already—had felt it yesterday beneath her fingers when he'd lifted her from her faint.

Great arms, terrific shoulders. Nice throat. Firm, male chin that—if she squinted—she could see was faintly stubbled. That mouth again and, oh, it was a good mouth—firm, powerful, masculine yet sensitive.

She heard herself give a little sigh. His nose that was uniquely his, not exactly straight—and she remembered something about a rugby injury years ago—but not too crooked either.

And those eyes. . . Poppy blanched. Those eyes were looking straight at her, and not just looking—glaring—spitting cold blue exasperation in her direction.

Immediately she lowered her gaze, staring at the small hands that twisted frantically in her lap, her pulse going ker-thump, ker-thump, ker-thump with panic.

'Dr Brown, perhaps you have a suggestion?'

She had been listening; she was sure she'd been listening, but somehow at the end there she'd been so engrossed in her examination of him that she'd missed his words. The sound of her name jerked her attention back, but she knew that it wasn't the first time he'd said them. Slowly she lifted her head. 'I—I'm sorry?'

You will be, said eyes that clearly knew she'd not been giving his talk her full attention. 'I asked if you could suggest a solution to your colleague's problem,' he said steadily.

'Um. . .?' She frowned, then said heavily, 'No.'

The room was very quiet and, apart from Tom's raised eyebrow, there was no movement. 'No?' he said—very quietly.

'That's right.' Poppy straightened in her chair, electing to brazen this out. 'I don't know.'

His face darkened but before he could say anything, Kim interrupted. 'I don't know either,' she said quickly. 'I know I must have learned about it some time but I don't remember. Perhaps you could explain, Tom, er. . . Mr Grainger?'

An uneasy rustle filtered through the room and Poppy realised that their fellow casualty officers were all looking at her and Kim strangely. She exchanged a stricken glance with the equally uncomfortable-looking Kim, then said unhappily, 'P-perhaps if you repeat the question?'

'Perhaps if you two start to listen,' he replied grimly. 'James asked if shift-swaps were possible.' He looked directly at Poppy, a look she tried to meet earnestly but, judging from the impatient twist of his mouth, she failed miserably. 'He needs someone to cover him for the first two hours of his evening shift on Thursday night, and as Derek has a surgical tutorial to attend that night we thought you might be amenable.'

'O-of course.' Poppy smiled weakly at the group, not remembering exactly which one was James. 'I'd be happy to.'

'Thank God for that.' After a brief, taut

second Tom's eyes veered away from hers and
he eased himself away from the desk. 'Right,
everybody. Let's practise what *some* of you
have just learned.'

The group filed out of the room after him,
Kim and Poppy at the rear. 'Thanks for trying,'
Poppy said under her breath, giving the blonde
girl a grateful smile. 'I guess you missed some
of that, too?'

'More or less,' Kim drawled. 'Hard to
imagine a woman keeping her mind on her work
when he's around, though. Great thighs, hmm?'

Poppy almost choked but she managed a
strangled, 'I hadn't noticed,' suspecting, from
Kim's knowing grin, that the words lacked con-
viction.

'And it's not just the way he looks. He's
so. . .commanding.' She gave a mock shiver,
her eyes dancing. 'Makes my toes curl. I feel
like a teenager again.'

Poppy knew exactly what she meant. Exactly.
What she wasn't sure about was how to deal
with that feeling.

CHAPTER FOUR

THE rest of the afternoon was spent rehearsing the trauma routine and learning their roles on the team and how to perform basic orthopaedic procedures. It was an engrossing session for which Poppy was grateful. Aside from vowing that the sooner she got this apology out of the way and got her reactions to Tom back on a normal footing the better, she had little time to dwell on anything but the training.

They were shown around the helicopter and given instruction on the use of the portable equipment it contained, and then they visited the trauma wards and Intensive Care Unit. Lucy had already told her that she'd been wrong the evening before to assume that the young man from the helicopter had died, and Poppy was pleased to see him doing well in ICU.

The session finished just before five, and while the rest of the group dispersed she and Derek returned to Casualty to complete the last hour of their shift. The registrars had been covering and the unit didn't seem especially busy, but Poppy saw a dozen patients with minor injuries before one of the other casualty officers arrived to relieve her at six.

Then, instead of immediately seeking out
Tom to attempt her grand apology, Poppy
acknowledged that her courage had dwindled
and she dawdled. She took her white coat to
the common-room, chatted with Derek about
his plans to sit his surgical exams and read all
the protocols on the notice-board. When she
checked her watch again it was almost six-
thirty.

By now she was alone in the room and she
allowed herself a small sigh. 'Too late,' she
said under her breath, for Derek had told her
that Tom was due to finish at six. She tried to
pretend that she felt real regret. 'You'll just
have to wait until tomorrow.'

Her movements jaunty now, she collected her
bag and coat and walked towards the half-open
door. 'And you absolutely have to stop talking
to yourself.'

But as she danced out she came smack up
against a broad chest, and for the second time
in as many days her head jerked up and she
met Tom's irritated look with horror. She
stepped back and then froze, registering the
sheaf of papers in his hand and realising that
he'd been about to deliver them to the common-
room. 'Oh,' she said, watching him drop the
papers onto the nearest desk, 'I was just. . .'

'Talking to yourself?' he offered grittily.

'Childhood habit,' she mumbled.

'I know.' He swivelled towards the door again. 'I remember.'

Poppy was flushing. Quickly, though, she stepped in front of him to stop him leaving. 'A-actually, I wanted to find you,' she said jerkily, shutting the door. 'I—I thought we might. . .discuss things.'

He frowned at the closed door. 'What sort of things?'

'I mean it's so long since I've seen you and there's so much I need to say. . .' She bit her lip, conscious that this wasn't going very well. 'Well, so much that I should have said before.'

Tom leaned back against the desk, his expression wary. 'Is this anything to do with work?'

'Oh, no, nothing to do with that.' The stiffening of his face made her even more nervous. She took a deep breath and lifted a self-conscious hand to smooth her hair, although it was so tightly coiled that not a single strand had escaped. 'No, this is. . .personal. Tom, I think it's time you knew how much I—'

'Poppy I'd like to think we can establish a good working relationship.'

'I'd like that too,' she said huskily, 'but—'

'A purely professional relationship,' he said firmly.

Poppy blinked. 'Yes, but first——'

'Do you remember what I said to you that night you came to my flat at St John's?'

Her mouth dropped open. 'M-most of it,' she admitted, not understanding where this conversation was going but knowing that she'd never forget the gentle but earth-shattering speech which had finally made her realise that her love for him was doomed.

'Then we understand each other,' he said flatly.

They did?

He gave her a hard look and then one hand at her shoulder levered her firmly aside and he opened the door. 'If you think about it carefully, you'll agree. This is a very important time in your career. My advice is to concentrate on your work.'

And suddenly, just as he'd left, she really did understand what he'd thought she'd meant—understood everything. 'No!' She gasped, mortified, her face flooding with colour again, for this was all her fault. After the way she'd been looking at him this afternoon no wonder he'd misunderstood.

Violently she wrenched the door open. 'Tom! Wait! It isn't like that.'

He was only a few yards away and when he turned she choked, 'I wasn't. . .I mean I'm not interested in you. . .like that.' He was waiting, his expression watchful, and she stumbled through an explanation. Oh, dear. This was awful! 'You're handsome, of course,' she rambled, barely aware of what she was saying and knowing only that she had to convince him that he was wrong.

'Handsome in a. . .mature way, and I'm sure women find you attractive but you're far too old for me and. . .' she searched desperately for more '. . .and you don't have to worry about me embarrassing you because, you see, I. . .I prefer my men blond.'

He'd started walking back towards her and when she said that he stopped. 'Your *men*?' he said softly, his voice tinged with incredulity.

Poppy nodded, clutching the doorhandle for support as her legs felt like they might crumble otherwise. 'All my men,' she said carefully, 'have been blond. That's what I like.'

'Really?' He folded his arms and leaned back against the corridor wall, his head tilted as if she suddenly intrigued him. 'When you say "men",' he said quietly, 'are we talking two, three. . .?' When she didn't say anything his regard sharpened. 'A dozen or more?'

She shifted uneasily from one foot to the

other. 'Something like that,' she said vaguely, wondering what sort of figure made a good average. 'The memories blur. You know how it is.'

'I thought I did,' he murmured, 'but it seems I was wrong.'

For a few seconds there was silence and then he added, 'So Poppy Brown's grown into a seductress. I suppose the signs were always there.'

She flushed at his mockery. '*Seductress* is a little extreme,' she said jerkily. She smoothed her hair with a hand that shook so much that she was surprised it didn't rattle. 'Actually, I'd rather not talk about this,' she said. 'It seems a little inappropriate, discussing my sex life with. . .'

'Someone so old?' he offered, his eyes narrowing at her relieved nod.

She managed a weak smile. 'After all, I work for you,' she added. 'We want to establish a good. . .' She paused, trying to remember his exact words. ' "Working relationship"—wasn't that what you suggested?'

The hardening of his mouth suggested that he didn't like having his own words mouthed back at him. 'Just as long as your *activities* don't interfere with your work,' he said coldly, levering himself away from the wall. 'Eight o'clock sharp tomorrow. I don't care how many blond men you seduce tonight—don't sleep in.'

She stared after him, her relief at his disappearance and his apparent belief of what she'd said tempered by her annoyance at the unfairness of his final comment and the dreadful knowledge that she'd still not been able to apologise to him.

Poppy didn't actually sleep in the next morning—well, not more than an extra fifteen minutes or so—but when her mother phoned as she was about to leave her nerves tensed.

Poppy had to tell her all about her new job, and once her mother discovered that Jeremy's medical school friend was her new consultant she refused to listen to Poppy's protestations that he'd be cross if she was late.

'Such a nice boy,' her mother said, delighted that Tom was now her daughter's boss. 'Always so organised. And a very good rugger player. Your father was very impressed with him, you remember, that game where Jeremy's arm was broken?'

Poppy lied and said she didn't remember but her mother rambled on, regardless. After several minutes of conversation she said, 'Bring Tom home one weekend, why don't you, Poppy? We'd love to see him again.'

'He's my consultant, mother, not my "chum".'

'Darling, don't be silly,' she was chided. 'He's a family friend. Jeremy's free at Easter. Why not invite Tom, too?'

Because Tom would have a million other things to do and Poppy would never get up the nerve to suggest it to him, but she muttered something vaguely acquiescent—anything to end the conversation—then said a determined goodbye, hanging up before her mother could protest.

She tore across the road to the hospital's main entrance, her fingers trying to pin her hair as she ran. The foyer was choked with staff and patients queuing for breakfasts at McDonald's and it took her several minutes to push her way through. By the time she finally arrived in Casualty, panting and dishevelled, it was almost eight-thirty.

Tom, of course, noted her arrival. 'Another fair-haired man too good to leave?' he asked acidly, his cool eyes surveying her flustered face.

Poppy squirmed, her worldly bravado of the evening before having long since evaporated. 'Sorry,' she mumbled. 'Majors or minors today?'

He reached for an enormously thick set of

notes and, as if annoyed by her refusal to deny his accusation, shoved them roughly in her direction. 'Just arrived. Cubicle two. Known asthmatic and chronic airways disease.'

Poppy took the files and turned hurriedly away, flicking through them as she walked quickly towards the cubicle, conscious that her face was still burning.

Fifty-eight-year-old Ray Powers sat hunched forward on the stretcher, his nicotine-stained fingers clutching at the edge of the bars, his breathing audibly wheezy, his chest heaving with effort and his colour grey.

'Mr Powers, I'm Dr Brown. What's been happening to you?'

The man glared at her. 'You're the doctor...aren't you?' he puffed between wheezes, looking resentfully at the notes she held. 'You...tell me.'

Her smile fixed, she skimmed the summaries of his last two attendances. Asthma since childhood, complicated and now overshadowed by severe smoking-related chronic airways disease. Three admissions in three years requiring ventilation. Problems exacerbated by aggression, non-compliance with medication, not attending outpatient appointments and continuing to smoke heavily. Frequent relapses post-discharge, several discharges against advice. 'What's brought this attack on?' she asked neutrally. 'Cough, cold—anything like that?'

He grunted, turning his head away from her so that she could see the muscles in his neck jerking with the effort he needed to breathe. 'Where's that. . .bloody nurse. . .with the nebuliser?'

Poppy sighed. 'Mr Powers, please. It's very important you talk to me.'

'Look, girlie,' he snarled, as much as it was possible to snarl when he could barely speak, 'give. . .me the stuff. . .and I'll be on. . .my way. Right?'

Acknowledging that she could hardly force him to give her a history, she explained that she needed to examine him. While he didn't co-operate he at least didn't refuse, and she checked his heart and lungs, registering the tachycardia and jump in his blood pressure when he breathed in which suggested that this was a severe attack.

He turned his head away with a fierce grimace when she offered him the peak flow meter and she put it aside, exchanging a strained look with the nurse who'd just arrived with a plastic ampoule of salbutamol for the nebuliser. 'Five milligrams in five millilitres, thanks. I'll be back in a few minutes.'

While she waited for the bronchodilator to take effect she saw the next patient on the board, a nineteen-year-old with an injured right knee which looked very much like a ruptured anterior cruciate ligament.

Mr Powers wasn't looking very much better when she returned. Despite the bronchodilator he'd finished, his chest still heaved with the effort of exhaling. He scowled at her but didn't object when she listened to his chest again. 'I want to do a blood test,' she said firmly, tugging across the trolley that held the syringes and needles.

He pulled his jacket across his chest and held it closed. 'No.'

'Mr Powers, it's very important that I know how much oxygen—'

Pointedly he told her where she could put her needle.

Poppy gripped the edge of the bed. 'Mr Powers—'

'Get me. . .another. . .nebuliser,' he said angrily, and to her relief she saw that his temper had added some colour to his complexion.

'In a minute. First—'

'I know. . .my rights,' he barked. 'You can't. . .touch me.'

Worried that the stress of arguing with her might make his breathing worse, Poppy closed

the curtains on him then hesitated. He might be
bad-tempered but there was nothing in the notes
to suggest any psychiatric disorder. Then again
he was a heavy smoker with chronic airways
disease so he'd be hypoxic and that could cause
aggression. Shouldn't she be doing more to find
out? But if he resisted a blood test what could
she do?

She was standing there, wondering, when the
staff nurse reappeared. She gave Poppy a sympathetic look. 'Another nebuliser?'

Poppy nodded. 'Better add in five hundred
of Atrovent,' she instructed, writing the prescription on the casualty card. She looked up,
frowning. 'Do you know him?'

The nurse rolled her eyes. 'I've seen him
worse,' she said quietly. 'Nine times out of ten
the doctors can't get near him. He just takes
his nebulisers and goes. He has to be nearly
unconscious before he agrees to admission.'

'But that's terrible!' Poppy was shocked.
'There's a treatable component to his disease.
We should be able to prevent some of this—
the asthma side, anyway.'

The older woman merely shrugged then vanished behind the curtains, and seconds later
Poppy heard the moist bubbling of the nebuliser
again.

Before returning to check on him, she saw

two other cases. After checking the X-rays from the man with the sore knee she referred him to the orthopaedic team.

The referral took longer than she'd expected and when she returned to Mr Powers he was obviously preparing to leave. His condition had mildly improved but he was by no means over his attack, his breathing still wheezy, and Poppy tried to stop him. 'You're not well enough to leave yet,' she said determinedly. 'You need admission.'

He swore, bending to collect a worn duffle bag from beneath the trolley.

'Even if you won't stay in hospital you need at least one more nebuliser,' she said. 'And a course of steroids. Otherwise you'll be back in a few hours.'

Apart from an angry grunt, he ignored that, pushing past her out of the cubicle and forcing her to chase after him. 'Mr Powers, you have to let me give you some steroids.'

But despite his asthma he managed to put a fair bit of distance between them, and she had to hurry to catch him up. 'What about your GP?' she demanded, reaching out an arm to grab for his sleeve. 'Will you see him?'

The reply to that was colourful, and although he was quite a small man he was strong enough to force her arm aside as he headed for the exit, attracting the attention of several dozen interested patients who were sitting in the waiting room.

'Inhalers?' she shouted, remembering the two devices which had been left untouched in the cubicle. 'You haven't taken your inhalers!'

But he was already gone and she sagged against the nursing station where Lucy was sorting through notes and X-rays. 'He's gone.' She dumped the notes onto the desk. 'Probably be brought in dead later.'

The sister squeezed her arm and smiled kindly. 'I haven't seen Ray Powers move that quickly in ten years.'

'He had fifteen millimetres of pulsus paradoxus,' Poppy said grimly. 'I should have tied him to the bed.'

Tom dumped several sets of notes onto the desk, exchanged a telling look with Lucy and said simply, 'Ray?'

Lucy nodded. 'Done a runner. As usual.'

'No doubt horribly hypoxic,' Poppy continued. 'I should never have let him walk out of here.'

Tom said, 'I doubt there was any "let" about it.' He took the file Lucy then offered him, his eyes on that rather than on Poppy. 'And that man's been hypoxic for twenty years. Did you check his saturations on the oximeter?'

'I didn't even think about it,' she said faintly, cursing herself. The machine would only have given a rough estimate of his oxygen levels but at least it would have been painless. 'He wouldn't let me do a blood gas but I didn't think of the oximeter.'

Tom shrugged, as if he was not overly concerned, but Poppy was furious with herself. If she'd proved that his oxygen level was too low for him to think rationally she might have had grounds for insisting that he stayed. 'Perhaps I can still get him back.' Quickly she flicked his notes open again. 'I'll call his GP. I'll ask him or her to go and——'

'Sorry.' Lucy's smile was resigned as she pointed to the almost blank data sheet Poppy was studying. 'No GP. No known address. No relatives.'

Poppy's shoulders sagged again. 'Oh.'

'He'll be back.' Tom was looking at her now——looking at her, she realised, with a sort of analytical curiosity as if her reaction interested him.

Her face suddenly flushed, she faltered, 'But what if he's. . .much worse?'

'You did your best at the time.' His gaze returned to the file he was holding. 'That's all any of us can do. The man doesn't want help. We can't force it on him.'

'If he's really hypoxic we could section him for treatment.'

'He's not psychotic.'

But Poppy didn't let it rest. 'I can't just allow him——'

He slammed the notes closed and looked at her again, his expression already back to the mingled exasperation and irritation with which he normally seemed to view her. 'You can't save the world, Poppy Brown.' He shoved the file roughly under his arm. 'And in the meantime there's work to be done.'

She stared after him, her eyes wide, and Lucy, too, seemed startled. 'Wonder what's eating him lately,' she mused, her brow creased as she twisted to watch his departure. 'He's normally so. . .calm.'

But Poppy had a fair idea what—or more precisely, *who*—was bothering him, and her fists clenched as she acknowledged that the pathetic mess she'd made of her apology last night had done little to improve his regard of her. 'Probably his mid-life crisis,' she said absently.

Lucy blinked. 'He's a little young.'

'Happens at all ages.' Poppy spoke distractedly, too much on her mind now to listen to herself properly. She was worried about Ray Powers. She was worried about Tom, and how they were not getting on. She wondered about how else she might try to make amends to him, and she worried especially about the little bubbles of hurt that had started to fizz up inside her at his rough departure.

'Do you know much about mid-life crises?' asked Lucy.

'I've studied psychiatry,' said Poppy, knowing that she couldn't admit the real reason for Tom's bad temper since she'd started the attachment. It wasn't just the past; he liked order and calm and he thought she was disrupting that. 'He's showing all the symptoms.'

The sister's mouth formed a rounded 'O' and then she was nodding. 'You know, I think you might be right,' she said thoughtfully. 'Is there anything we should be doing to help him?'

Poppy frowned vaguely, still preoccupied. Perhaps she should put her apology in writing? That way she might be able to convey her real feelings, her regret, without it being ruined by embarrassing misunderstandings or by her becoming tongue-tied in front of him.

'Poppy?' Lucy was prompting her again. 'Is there anything we should be doing to help Tom with this?'

'Um. . .' Poppy hesitated. Help Tom? How should they help Tom? 'Be nice,' she improvised finally. 'Be. . .gentle and supportive.'

How wonderful it would be if he was gentle and supportive towards her. Perhaps he'd return the favour? 'Show him that we care,' she added. 'That we're there for him if he needs us. Be kind.'

'I'll pass the word around.' Lucy tucked a few strands of short blonde hair behind her ear and stood, collecting the folders and X-rays she'd sorted. 'We'll look after him, make sure he doesn't work too hard.'

Poppy took the next file in the box. 'Drown him in kindness.'

The door to the paediatric room was open, and as she walked past she saw Tom crouch and look into a small child's ear with an otoscope. The easy movement highlighted the muscular strength of his thighs and she caught her breath, once again forced to acknowledge the powerful male appeal of him.

'This is all in your head,' she told herself fiercely, dragging her eyes away. 'For God's sake, pull yourself together before he catches you and you're out on the street.'

Rushing through the hospital foyer next morning, Poppy very nearly tripped over the outstretched legs of a tall doctor who was sitting outside McDonald's drinking coffee. He saw her stumble, they both apologised and then she hurried on her way—but not before noticing his very blond hair.

That triggered thoughts of her embarrassing discussion with Tom about blond men, and Poppy winced at the memory of his expression when he'd thought she was propositioning him. She had to do more to convince him that she saw him purely as her boss. 'Which is perfectly true,' she said firmly. 'You've learned your lesson as far as Tom Grainger's concerned.'

But it didn't help that she could barely keep her eyes off him. Too often she was catching herself watching him and that was dangerous. Sooner or later he was going to notice. From the hard looks he'd been giving her it was even possible that he'd noticed already, and until she had these. . .odd emotions she was experiencing under control she needed to keep him distracted.

'Blond men,' she vowed. She pushed open the doors to Casualty and looked expectantly around majors, relieved—despite her vow— that the only man in sight was a bald porter.

Tom sent her to minors for the morning, but after lunch it was quiet so she went to see if she was needed in majors. As soon as she walked in she saw Lucy, her hands solidly on her hips, confronting Tom. Judging from the determined set of the sister's face, they'd been arguing.

'Tell him, Poppy,' Lucy said crossly, sending

her a relieved look which suggested that she thought she'd found an ally. 'Tell him it's not healthy to eat lunch on the job. He needs a proper break.'

Poppy blinked, saw Tom's glowering exasperation and paled at the memory of Lucy's concern about Tom's fictional mid-life crisis. 'Not taking a proper break is unhealthy,' she said mechanically.

'You're worse than my four-year-old,' Lucy scolded him. 'Stubborn as a mule. For heaven's sake, we'll cope without you for half an hour. Go!'

Tom's brow darkened ominously. 'You both seem to have forgotten,' he said tightly, 'that *I'm* in charge of this department.'

'The mental health of staff is my concern, too.' Lucy's briskness startled Poppy, who'd never have guessed that the gentle sister had such a thread of steel. 'Go to lunch.'

Tom's expression turned thunderous and Poppy groaned. She shuffled backwards but Lucy wasn't about to let her escape. 'Tell him, Poppy. Tell him he has to go.'

Poppy focused on Tom's beautifully knotted tie. 'L-Lucy's right,' she said finally. 'We'll manage. I'll help here.'

'You think that's reassuring?' he snapped.

Prepared to concede her inexperience but

confident about her competence, Poppy bristled. In a major emergency there was back-up available, and he carried a trauma bleeper if they needed him. 'You're not indispensable,' she said shrilly. 'The world's not about to fall apart because you take a lunch-break.'

'Poppy's right.' Lucy spoke hurriedly. 'Even if you don't like it, you know she's right.'

'Poppy Brown is not in charge of this department.'

'Perhaps she should be.' Lucy was determined now. Ignoring his irritation, she wrenched open the double doors. 'She's much more sensible than you. Out. Now. Lunch.'

Tom's obvious astonishment at hearing Poppy described as 'sensible' cut right through his anger. For one stunned moment he simply stared at the defiant sister, swallowed, gave Poppy a brief, hard look and then to her relief merely muttered, 'Lunch,' as if the issue had never been in dispute. 'Back in thirty minutes.'

When the doors swung shut behind him Poppy expelled the breath she'd been holding and met Lucy's satisfied nod with a weak smile.

'He works too hard,' the sister said briskly. 'At this rate, even if he gets over this crisis thing, he'll have a heart attack before he's forty.' She looked pointedly at Poppy. 'Time he got himself married.'

Poppy studied the tetanus-prevention poster behind Lucy's head. 'I—I'm sure he's not short of offers.'

'He needs someone who'll shake him up. That man is far too used to getting his own way.'

Poppy pictured Tom's reaction to match-making attempts by Lucy, murmured something indistinct about tetanus and fled.

Later she saw him arrive back from lunch but managed to stay out of his way for much of the afternoon, which was not difficult as a steady stream of patients kept all of them fully occupied. Also, it was as though she had radar as far as he was concerned. She could *feel* where he was, even when she couldn't see him, and although that sensitivity worried her at least it simplified avoiding him.

Shortly before six she lifted her hand to the back of her neck, trying to rub away her tiredness. Although she'd been working for almost ten hours she'd agreed to cover the first two hours of the evening shift for James and so wasn't due to finish until eight.

She stretched, arching her back, then felt the hairs on her arm prickle. Straightening abruptly, she turned and caught Tom watching her.

Immediately he turned into a cubicle, but not before she'd caught the unguarded speculation in his eyes. She flushed, dropped her eyes hastily back to her notes and wondered what had caused that look, alarmed by the sudden pounding of her heart.

She slammed the file shut and reached for a new one, glancing at the cubicle number before striding towards it. 'If you don't pull yourself together you'll be out of a job by the end of the week.' She pulled the curtains around the trolley, trying not to notice the way her hands were shaking. 'You know he won't put up with you mooning over him.'

She summoned a self-conscious smile for the dishevelled young man who sat perched on the trolley, watching her interestedly. Obviously he'd overheard her comment. 'It's all right,' Poppy said weakly, 'I'm not mad.' Well, not yet anyway. 'I'm the doctor.'

As if worried about eavesdroppers, his glittering eyes shifted uneasily around the cubicle. 'I understand,' he hissed, tapping the side of his nose. 'Aliens.' His eyes darted to the ceiling. 'They talk to me, too.'

Poppy swallowed, jarred by the memory of her panic-stricken flight from Green Ward on her first day at the hospital. Hastily she checked the diagnosis on the file she was holding.

Vaginal discharge. Pelvic infection. 'Sorry, wrong cubicle,' she said tightly, retreating fast. 'Your doctor will be along shortly.'

She pulled the curtain shut sharply and grimaced. She really *had* to stop talking to herself.

Tom's low voice brought her head up. 'Friend of yours?' he drawled.

Poppy tensed. 'I. . .he's the wrong patient.' She looked at the white-board behind him and saw from the green 'T' and red 'P' that Tom had already seen the man she'd just visited and had referred him to the duty psychiatrist. She held up the file. 'Miss Waterstone?'

'Gynae cubicle,' he said flatly. 'But feel free to talk with my patient. You may find you share a delusion or two.'

Poppy coloured. 'I told you that day I was very tired—'

'And overwrought.' The corners of his mouth lifted. 'Not to mention panic-stricken into such a state of hysteria that you collapsed at my feet.'

'You're exaggerating,' she said stiffly, looking past him towards the white-board, her eyes on the blond male doctor who'd appeared in front of it. Very blond, she noted, like the one at McDonald's this morning, not sure if she was happy about that or not. Still, she was hardly likely to get a better opportunity, not one with Tom so handy. Steeling herself, she widened her eyes and asked sweetly, 'Who's that?'

Tom followed her gaze. 'Psych SR. For your friend.'

Poppy let her eyes make a leisurely inspection of the registrar. 'Nice.'

'Why not tell him about your aliens?' he said coolly. 'I'm sure he'd be interested. They section people for less.'

Poppy ignored that. 'Is he married?'

'No.' He tapped the file she held close to her chest. 'Aren't you forgetting Miss Waterstone?'

But Poppy was determined to make this convincing. 'In a minute,' she said, her voice carefully distracted.

She approached the registrar with trepidation for she had no idea how to appear completely businesslike to him while looking like an experienced woman bent on seduction from where Tom was standing. 'Dr Rogers?' she said huskily, reading the badge pinned to his suit. 'Poppy Brown. How do you do?'

He looked puzzled but he put aside the notes he was reading to shake her hand. 'Mike Rogers. I thought this referral came from Tom?'

'It does.' Conscious of Tom standing a few feet behind, she tossed her head but realised too late that her hair was too tightly coiled to move. 'But I wanted to introduce myself,' she drawled, wincing inwardly. 'Do you. . .come here often?'

Mike Rogers looked bemused. He pushed his round spectacles higher on his nose. 'Fairly,' he said faintly. 'Er. . . I'd better see my patient.'

'Perhaps we'll chat later?'

His throat make a convulsive movement. 'Perhaps.' She saw him exchange a quick panicked look with Tom and then he vanished behind the curtain of his patient's cubicle.

Tom seemed to be enjoying himself. 'Too *femme fatale* for Mike,' he advised. 'You frightened him.'

She'd frightened herself. 'He'll be back,' she muttered as she escaped.

Fifteen minutes later when she re-emerged from the gynae cubicle there was no sign of Tom, and the psychiatric patient and registrar had disappeared too, presumably to somewhere that offered more privacy than the curtained cubicle.

Relieved, for Poppy was sure that she'd made a fool of herself in front of all of them, she busied herself packaging up the swabs she'd taken from her patient and writing her a prescription for some antibiotics.

Chasing other men when Tom was around to prove that she wasn't interested in him was not the brightest idea she'd had this week, she acknowledged.

One of the senior staff nurses looked over her shoulder. 'PID?'

Poppy nodded. 'I think so. She's not too bad but I'm starting the antibiotics anyway, awaiting the microbiology.'

'The gynae people like to review all suspected cases once the results are back. Want me to ask Reception to make an appointment?'

'Please.' She signed her notes with a flourish and handed them across. 'Er. . . Tom's finished, I suppose?' she asked airily.

'Hounded out the door by Lucy,' the older woman confirmed. 'First day he's left on time since he started.' She laughed. 'He wasn't happy about it either.'

'Oh?'

'Lucy's convinced he's working himself into a nervous breakdown. At hand-over she told us to treat him *kindly*!' She shook her head. 'Poor man doesn't stand a chance. The young ones are already falling over each other fetching him cups of tea and offering him back rubs—and more.'

Poppy smiled nervously. 'He does seem a bit tense,' she suggested tentatively.

The nurse snorted. 'Tense?' she scoffed. 'Another few days of fussing and he'll be tense all right. But it won't be anything to do with work—this job's a doddle for the likes of him.'

She laughed again. 'I tell you what, though, he's a man who likes to be in control. There'll be fun and games when he discovers the reason for all this attention.'

Poppy visualised Tom's reaction and blanched. Expressing doubts about the stability of her boss's mental health had been another major error of judgement recently. She slid off her stool. 'On with the work,' she said stiffly. 'Anything interesting?'

'Tricyclic overdose in Resusc. Fully conscious. If you see her first I'll organise this appointment and be back in a few minutes to help wash her out.'

By eight, when James arrived to take over his shift, the girl had had her stomach washed out, then filled up with charcoal and had been referred to the medical team. Although she'd taken the tablets to frighten her estranged boyfriend, rather than to commit suicide, she'd taken enough so that among other things the drug could potentially affect her heart rhythm and so she needed to be monitored overnight.

Poppy briefly ran over the remainder of the patients she'd seen who were still in the department, either awaiting results or under observation in the small casualty side ward. 'And there's a chap I saw this morning, severe COAD, who might be back,' she told him, explaining about Mr Powers. 'I've been expecting him all afternoon.'

'Fine.' James noted the details in a notebook. Then he lowered his voice. 'Before you go,' he murmured, 'what's this I hear about Tom cracking up?'

Poppy stiffened. 'What?'

'Giles in minors said he overheard some nurses from the trauma ward talking in the McDonald's queue,' he explained. 'Apparently they've heard their new consultant's a fruit cake.' He frowned. 'Well, that's Tom, isn't it?'

Poppy blinked. Oh, dear. 'I—I think so,' she stammered. 'Unless they've appointed another one.'

'These nurses said that some doctor who's an expert on male mid-life disorders or something crazy like that thinks he's borderline psychotic,' he added.

'R-really?'

'You've been working with him,' James persisted. 'Does he seem OK to you?'

'F-fine,' she said shakily. How could she have been so...irresponsible? She knew how rumours could spread like Chinese whispers through hospitals—particularly rumours about Tom! 'He's fine,' she repeated rawly. 'Fine.'

He slanted her a doubtful look. 'You don't sound sure.'

'Of course I'm sure,' she squeaked. 'It's probably a joke. A stray comment from someone...' She sucked her cheeks. 'You know what hospitals are like.'

'He certainly seems pretty stable,' James acknowledged. 'There must be another trauma consultant.'

Poppy looked around nervously. 'I wouldn't mention this to anyone else,' she said quietly. 'The less said the better.'

James accepted that with a firm nod, then glanced at his watch. 'Thanks for covering. See you tomorrow.'

Poppy hurried back to the dingy flat which the hospital's accommodation department had allocated her. Although she was tired, her body hummed with nervous tension and she found it impossible to relax. It was after midnight before she made it into bed, very worried. How on earth was she going to extricate herself from the mess she'd created?

CHAPTER FIVE

IT WAS a tired and miserable Poppy who struggled through the crowds queuing at McDonald's and dragged herself into the casualty department on Friday morning.

She went directly to the common-room to fetch her white coat, nodding a greeting to Derek who was hard at work with his surgical text again.

He blinked at her. 'Aren't you in Theatres this morning?'

Poppy frowned. 'Theatres?'

He pointed to one of the notices on the board. '"Intubation training. Dr Brown, main theatres, seven-thirty." Today's date. Didn't you see this?'

A bell jangled vaguely in her head but she hesitated. This morning she wanted to stay in Casualty: she had to work on limiting the damage her stupid stories about Tom had caused. She had to talk urgently to Lucy and explain that she hadn't been serious. 'Derek. . .?' She eyed her colleague speculatively. 'How about swapping——?'

'Dr Brown?' Tom's voice sliced through her

113

request and Poppy froze, not brave enough to look at him.

'I've had one of the anaesthetists on the telephone, asking what's happened to his SHO this morning,' he continued grimly. 'Knowing your. . .distaste for punctuality, I presume that doctor is you?'

'On my way,' she said stiffly. She turned her head slowly, dared one brief look at him and winced. 'I'm sorry,' she said, promptly remembering how much she had to apologise for. 'Really sorry. For everything.'

Tom blinked, then said grudgingly, 'It's only thirty minutes. It might have been worse.'

'Believe me, I never meant it to go this far,' she mumbled. Hopefully he'd remember those words when he discovered how she'd been gossiping about him. 'Anything you hear about, please accept that I'm sorry. Sorry. Sor—'

'Poppy, get upstairs,' he snapped, his glare pure blue exasperation. 'And, for God's sake, don't apologise to anyone up there. They'll be sending for the psychiatrists!'

'Sorry,' she said quickly, ducking under his arm. Now that she'd actually said the word it felt as if the weight of the world had been lifted off her shoulders. Apologising really wasn't that difficult. She smiled.

But she wasn't smiling as she stalked back to Casualty that afternoon, still wearing theatre blues and white theatre clogs, hair that had been neatly braided now loosened and tousled from the elasticised paper hat she'd had to wear all morning.

Lucy was munching chicken nuggets in the tearoom and Poppy glared at her balefully. 'Someone stole my suit from Theatre changing rooms,' she said mournfully. 'My brand new suit.'

Lucy looked astonished. 'Someone stole that tweedy thing?'

'And my shoes.' Poppy grimaced. 'I only bought them on Monday.'

The sister's mouth twitched but her voice, when she spoke, was warm with concern. 'You've told Security?'

'I gave them a drawing of it.' She didn't dwell on the disbelief with which the head of security had greeted her careful artistic effort. 'They're checking the security cameras at the hospital exits.'

'Never mind, Poppy. I'm sure they'll turn up.' Lucy gave her a reassuring smile. 'And even if they don't. . .' She hesitated. 'You know I'd normally never say anything but really that outfit didn't do you justice. You're too slender to wear something so old and shapeless—it

looked like it was drowning you. And those
shoes. . .' She shuddered, clearly enjoying
herself now. 'Those shoes were the sort grand-
mothers wear. And those tights——'

'Lucy!' Enough was enough and Poppy
scowled at the sister, affronted. She'd grown
fond of the comfortable suit, and the brogues
had been softening slowly, *and* neither had been
cheap. 'For your information——'

'What's all the noise?' Tom brushed past
Poppy, silencing her and sending tingles of
shivery sensation spinning along her arm.

'Someone stole Poppy's new suit,' Lucy said
promptly. 'From Theatres. And her shoes.'

'Really?' Tom took the chair beside Lucy,
lifting a burger out of a McDonald's paper bag.
'They must have been desperate.'

Lucy's giggle drowned out Poppy's outraged
gasp. 'I told her it didn't flatter her,' Lucy
explained. 'Even that smock's better, don't you
think?'

To Poppy's distress, Tom seemed to give the
issue serious consideration. 'Pity about the head
full of bubbles,' he said finally.

'Tom!' Lucy looked shocked. 'You can't talk
about your SHOs like that. Poppy's very
bright.'

'Do you mind?' Poppy scowled at the pair
of them. 'I am still here, you know!'

'Hard to forget,' Tom drawled. 'Much as we'd like to.'

'For your information, my last consultant told me I was the best house officer he'd ever had,' she said tightly. 'He said I'd go far!'

'He meant he *hoped* you'd go far,' Tom countered. 'Far away!'

Poppy's eyes narrowed. 'For your further information, out of the ninety students in my final year I was ranked fifth!'

'In what?' he demanded, letting his burger slide back into its bag, all his attention on her now. It felt like a declaration of war. 'Delusions of grandeur?'

'Tom!' Lucy's appalled exclamation tightened the tension that stretched between the two doctors. 'Whatever personal upheaval you're going through, you can't take it out on Poppy. She hasn't done anything wrong.'

Tom stiffened and the air hummed with electricity. '*Personal upheaval*?'

Poppy winced. 'Leave it, Lucy,' she said quickly. 'Not now.'

But Tom held up his hand. 'Yes, now!' Narrowed eyes flicked suspiciously to Poppy. 'Spit it out, Lucy; I'm interested. Exactly what *personal upheaval* are you referring to?'

Lucy's mouth opened but Poppy said

urgently, 'Lucy, we need to talk first. I have to explain something!'

'Shut up, Poppy!' Tom's eyes were fixed on the sister. 'Come on, Lucy.' His voice was low and insistent and very quiet. 'Out with it.'

Poppy could see her career shattering around her ears. She felt dizzy and hot and the feelings gave her inspiration. Uttering a little cry, she pushed herself away from the door, twirled, then folded herself to the ground—face down, eyes closed.

'She's fainted!' Lucy's horrified exclamation was followed by firm, impatient hands, turning her over. 'Look! She's pale as a ghost!'

'It's her party trick.' Poppy winced at Tom's grasp at her ankles as he lifted her legs into the air. 'Gets her out of all sorts of trouble,' he added dryly.

After a few seconds Poppy let her eyes blink open. 'W-where am I?' she asked dazedly.

'In a hospital,' Tom said grimly, releasing her legs abruptly. This time she was ready for that and took the weight of them, lowering them to the floor more carefully than last time. 'We're going to admit you to the psychiatric ward.'

'Stop teasing her!' Lucy's worried face peered down. 'Poppy, are you all right?' she asked carefully. 'Is there something we should know?'

'She's not pregnant,' offered Tom. 'Although not through lack of opportunity.'

Poppy glared at him, knowing that she only had herself to blame for that, but unable to bite back a retort. 'You're hardly in a position to lecture me on sexual morals!'

'At least I have some!'

'Oh, yes?' She scrambled to her feet. 'I don't chase *married* men.'

Hard eyes bored into hers and she knew that he knew exactly what she was talking about. 'You know *nothing* about that,' he said softly. 'Nothing.'

But she remembered everything—Adele's kiss, their tumble on to the bed. 'I know what I saw,' she whispered.

'The whole world knows what you saw.' He looked exasperated and Poppy flinched. 'The best any of us can hope for is that the past six years have taught you to think before you open your mouth.'

Poppy paled, remembering that he was on the verge of discovering that she'd not learned that at all.

'Um. . .' Lucy's soft voice startled Poppy. Judging from Tom's sharp look, they'd obviously *both* forgotten her presence. The sister looked intrigued but she backed towards the door. 'You obviously have things to discuss. . .'

'Stay,' said Tom, forcibly. 'I'm leaving.' He stalked out of the room, leaving Poppy and Lucy staring at each other.

'Er. . . Tom and I have met before,' Poppy said lamely, clasping and unclasping her hands nervously. 'He was a registrar at St John's where I trained.' She took a deep breath. 'Lucy, you know the things I said about this mid-life crisis thing—'

Before she could explain one of the staff nurses popped her head around the room, smiled apologetically and said, 'Lucy, you haven't forgotten the meeting? It's gone two already.'

'Sorry.' Lucy gave Poppy a mysterious smile as she bustled out. 'I'm sure the two of you will sort things out,' she said vaguely.

Minors was busy all afternoon and the nurses doing triage and working with her were very experienced. Virtually all the cases were mild— earaches, sprained ankles, jammed fingers, broken collar-bones—so it wasn't particularly taxing intellectually and Poppy found herself replaying Tom's words over and over in her head.

His comment about hoping she'd learned to think before she spoke haunted her. How would he react when he discovered the things she'd been telling Lucy? She had to explain to the sister that she'd simply been playing a joke. But each time she managed to squeeze a few seconds spare to check majors she was told that Lucy was still away at her meeting.

On one occasion she even saw an exasperated Tom fending off a helpful nurse who was insisting that he needed his shoulders massaged, while another plied him with herbal tea. 'I do not need to relax,' Poppy heard him snap through gritted teeth and she fled back to minors, quivering.

At six Security called to say that they'd still not found her stolen clothing. 'Despite your. . . er. . .drawing,' the man said, so stiffly that she suspected he was suppressing giggles, 'which we've. . .er. . .pinned in a prominent place for all to see.'

Poppy grunted. 'But you'll keep looking?'

'Oh, we certainly will, Dr Brown. Count on us. If that. . .er. . .outfit walks out of here we'll be onto it.' There was a muffled sound that sounded suspiciously like a bark. 'Er. . .so to speak.'

'I'd appreciate it,' Poppy said formally, determined to retain her dignity—this time at least. 'I'll call after the weekend.'

She lowered the receiver with a sigh but consoled herself with the thought that even though

she couldn't afford to buy a replacement outfit
Tom clearly thought her hopeless anyway so
the disguise hadn't worked. She had nothing to
lose by reverting to her normal clothes.

When James arrived to relieve her he said,
'Your man, Powers, was back last night. Took
a couple of nebulisers and, remembering what
you said, I managed to persuade him to swallow
some prednisolone before he did another
runner.'

Poppy frowned. 'Was he all right?'

'Looked pretty grim,' he admitted. 'Terrified
you were going to be here—assuming that
you're the mad woman who chased him around
the department.'

'Well, if he could tell you that much he was
better,' she said, relieved. 'He could barely talk
yesterday morning.'

'He was talking, all right. Most of it
colourful.'

Poppy was smiling as she walked away. At
the back of her mind she'd been worried about
Mr Powers and, while everything else today had
been awful, at least he'd sounded a little better.

She went to find Lucy again but as she passed
the equipment room she heard Tom's voice,
tight with frustration. Unable to stop herself,
she pressed an ear to the door.

'And while I appreciate your nurses' thought-

fulness I do not need six cups of tea an hour,'
he was saying grimly. 'Nor do I need to sit and
rest or have my neck rubbed. I don't want them
to fetch me French fries and I certainly do not
want to discuss my problems. Lucy, has everyone here gone mad?'

Poppy sucked in her cheeks. Gingerly she
opened the door, wincing at Tom's accusing
glare.

'Poppy Brown,' he said wearily. 'What a surprise. Adding eavesdropping to your sins now?'

Poppy flushed. 'I was walking past and I
couldn't help but—'

'Overhear?' His smile was nasty. 'We gathered that. Do continue.'

She swallowed, fixing her gaze on Lucy.
'The other day,' she said shakily, 'I wasn't serious. About Tom. You remember. He's not in
the least. . .unstable.'

A frown furrowed Lucy's brow but Tom
spoke first, clicking his fingers irritably. 'Out
with it.'

She took a deep breath. 'You've been behav-
ing a little oddly.' She saw his darkening
expression and hurried on, 'I suggested that you
might be going through a mid-life crisis. I told
Lucy you needed support and. . .'

He scowled. 'And?'

'Kindness,' she said huskily. 'I told them to be kind.'

He sighed heavily. 'I've been plagued for three days because you, Poppy Brown, told these people to be *kind*?'

'Yes,' she said in a small voice, so small that it was almost inaudible. 'But I've already apologised. This morning, remember, I said sorry——'

'Lucy, will you leave us, please,' he said abruptly.

Lucy looked alarmed but Tom spoke again before she could say anything. 'No, we'll leave you,' he said grimly. He opened the door nearest Poppy. 'Collect your things. You're coming with me.'

Poppy pressed herself against the wall. 'Where are we going?'

'Nowhere pleasant,' he grated. 'Now move.'

One look into those determined eyes told her all she needed to know. He was furious and he was going to make her pay. She moved.

But not fast enough because, although she detoured only long enough to collect her bag, he caught up with her before she made it out of the department. From the way he'd been lounging near the exit door, she realised that he'd anticipated her frantic bid for freedom. 'Going somewhere?'

'Home,' she said huskily. 'It's after six. You can't stop me.'

'I think I can.' He took her arm and steered her into the dark evening and towards the car park. 'That is, if you want a job to come to on Monday morning.'

Poppy dragged her feet but he simply slowed his pace, his movements no less purposeful. 'I could lodge a complaint about this,' she muttered. 'This is sexual harassment.'

'I don't want to have sex with you,' he growled. 'I want to strangle you.'

'They'll find my body,' she said hoarsely, common sense telling her that he was joking but the tight set of his face leaving room for doubt. 'Lucy knows we left together.'

'She'll keep her mouth shut.' Narrowed blue eyes mocked her fear. 'And by the time I've finished there won't be a body to find.' He directed her to a large car which glinted silver under the orange lights of the car park. It looked vaguely like something her father used to drive although—as her knowledge of cars extended only to distinguishing her Honda from anything else in the car park—she didn't attempt to identify it further.

He unlocked the passenger door. 'Besides, after the things you've been saying they'll

assume I'm mad,' he said, bundling her inside
and shutting the door.

He strode around to the other side. 'I might
end up in Broadmoor for a year or two,' he
continued matter-of-factly, the name of the high
security psychiatric hospital tripping casually
off his tongue, 'before I stage a miraculous
recovery, but at the moment it seems worth it.'

Her mouth dried. 'Worth it?'

He was smiling as he started the car and
snapped on the lights. 'To be rid of you,' he
drawled, his fingers adjusting the heating control so that warm air began to blow towards her
chilled feet. 'To get my department back to
normal again. Put on your seat belt, Poppy. I
don't want you to get hurt *accidentally*.'

'You *are* mad,' she muttered, fumbling with
the strap. 'Completely mad.' She glanced at him
again as he reversed out of the car park. 'I
don't understand what's happened to you,' she
continued, knowing that she was babbling but
too nervous to stop. 'You used to be such a
nice person. Everyone thought so. Even my
mother said what a nice young man you were.
But Lucy's seen you at your worst now. Lucy
knows what a—'

'Which way?'

She looked up sharply. He'd stopped at the

car park exit and traffic was banking up behind them. 'What?'

He sighed. 'Which way do I turn?'

She looked vaguely from side to side. 'That depends on where you want to go, doesn't it?'

'Where do you live?' he grated.

She blinked. 'Where do I live?'

A car behind them hooted and Tom swore under his breath. 'Poppy—'

'Here, I live here,' she said quickly, for the rising colour in his face alarmed her. 'Here at the hospital.'

He swore again and she glared at him reproachfully. 'Ladies present,' she murmured, careful to keep the words under her breath.

One brief, hard look told her that he'd heard the comment and disputed it. Although his mouth tightened he didn't say anything, merely pulled smoothly out of the car park then re-entered at the next exit and parked in the spot he'd vacated.

He switched off the engine and there was silence. Poppy tugged at her doorhandle but it wouldn't move. She shifted in her seat and when he still didn't say anything she blurted, 'It's not my fault. If you'd told me where we were going before—'

'You can hardly go anywhere in those.' His eyes raked her theatre smock and clogs dismissively. 'You look like a child at a pyjama party.'

She sniffed. 'If I'm about to be strangled it hardly matters.'

He made a small choking sound. 'Don't you want to die looking glamorous?'

'No one would recognise me at my funeral.'

He climbed out of the car and then opened her door. 'Come on.'

'I'll change and come right back,' she assured him, scrambling out with as much dignity as she could considering that the wooden clogs were three sizes too large.

He took her arm firmly, as if he thought she might run for it. 'Best I come along and protect you,' he said smoothly. 'The aliens might come back.'

Once she'd mentioned aliens, she thought resentfully. Once. One little mention when she'd been frightened and distraught, yet he seemed obsessed with it. 'You know there's plenty of scientific evidence suggesting alien visitations,' she told him tersely as they crossed the road towards the hospital flats. 'But governments keep the information secret.'

'There's plenty of evidence to suggest that your head is, indeed, full of bubbles,' he countered, 'but I'll keep that a secret too.'

Poppy wrenched her arm free and promptly missed his touch. 'This way,' she snapped, directing him to the tattered concrete block to their left. 'Mind the puddles.'

It was a two-storeyed block containing twelve flats, each leading off a dimly lit and damp corridor. Poppy's flat was on the first floor, adjacent to a grimy stairwell.

She unlocked her door and grimaced at the musty smell that greeted them. She'd done her best to air the place, leaving the windows wide despite the cold whenever she was home, but according to her neighbours the burglary rate in the area was too high to risk leaving them ajar when she was at work.

Tom disparagingly inspected the dingy interior, with its peeling wallpaper and indifferent cheap furniture. 'I'd forgotten how awful hospital flats are in this country,' he said grimly. 'It's years since I've lived in one.'

Flushing faintly at the memory of his flat at St John's, Poppy dropped her bag onto the nearest chair. 'Unbelievably, this is supposed to be one of the better ones.' She stooped and lit the small gas fire which was the only source of heat in the room. For February the last week had been uncharacteristically warm but certainly not warm enough to manage without it, inadequate though it was. 'I didn't have much choice.'

Once the fire had taken she stood up awkwardly, brushing down her smock. The flat hadn't struck her as particularly small before, but with Tom here it was uncomfortably cramped. 'Um. . .tea?'

He winced. 'God, no! Any more tea and I'll sprout leaves.'

Poppy flushed again, remembering the way he'd complained to Lucy about all the tea. 'Tom, I'm really sorry about the mess I created,' she said quickly. 'I never meant—'

He lifted his hand. 'Poppy, just get changed.'

'Get it over with,' she said quietly. 'Yell at me, call me anything you want, whatever. I can take it.'

But he just sighed, then bent and retrieved a paperback she'd left beside the couch. 'Poppy, Poppy, Poppy,' he said wearily, his brows lifting as he studied the book's lurid cover— purple, white-eyed aliens emerging from a flying saucer. 'Can't you see half the fun's in the anticipation?'

'Half *your* fun,' she protested, her fingers itching to snatch the book away from him. 'None of mine.'

He shrugged. 'I'll wait here.' He opened the book. 'Take your time. This looks. . .interesting.'

'It would help,' she said tensely, 'if you told me where you were taking me.'

One broad shoulder lifted nonchalantly but

he seemed engrossed in the book, his voice distracted as he said, 'Somewhere we can talk without freezing to death.'

Somewhere he could tell her off, he meant. Poppy closed the bedroom door on him and slumped onto her bed, her mouth tightening as she immediately slid into the dip in the middle of the thin mattress.

It wasn't fair that he was so attractive, she thought wearily. It wasn't fair that while he was about to call her silly and irresponsible and thoughtless, all she could think about was the wonderful colour of his eyes and the male curve of his mouth. It wasn't fair that just being close to him turned her into the *bubble-headed* idiot he kept accusing her of being.

Although she tried pretending that she'd only come with him tonight because she was worried about keeping her job, that wasn't the real reason. Knowing that he was angry with her didn't dull the excitement she felt at being close to him, but merely gave their encounter an edge of danger that flickered at her nerves like an electric blade. 'Nothing's fair in this life,' she said sadly. 'Nothing.'

She wiggled her way out of the dip and back to her feet, struggled with the door of the built-in wardrobe which habitually jammed off its runners, finally wrenched it open and grimaced at the measly collection of clothes that hung inside.

When she returned to the sitting room he looked up from her book and blinked, his startled eyes widening as they took in her face.

Poppy stiffened. Without giving him time to speak, she retreated to her room and peered anxiously at her face, tilting the mirror to make the most of the poor light that filtered from her bedside lamp. She didn't normally wear make-up but tonight she'd experimented subtly with a few items she'd accumulated.

The lamp's pathetic beam made it hard to see anything so, keeping her head lowered, she opened the door again and raced past him to the bathroom. Shutting the door firmly behind her, she squinted into the tiny mirror above the cracked sink and groaned.

Subtle, it wasn't. Two hemispheres of fuchsia highlighted her cheeks, and the scarlet streak that was her mouth served only to make her freckles glow. The contrast with the red hair she'd bundled into a loose top-knot turned her clown-like. Furiously she dampened her face-cloth and scrubbed at her skin.

She sank weakly on to the edge of the bath. 'Idiot!' But after a few miserable minutes she acknowledged that there was little point in hiding in the bathroom—he wasn't exactly going to forget how she'd looked. Who *could* forget?

Stiffly she stalked through the living room directly to the front door and the woollen coat that hung on the back of it. Once she had herself firmly buttoned away she dared a look, relieved to see that while his brow was creased he didn't actually seem to be laughing at her. Perhaps she hadn't looked as awful as she'd thought? The thought was cheering. 'Ready?' she demanded archly.

With apparent reluctance he discarded the book, stood and then crouched to switch off the fire. 'You're very enthusiastic all of a sudden.'

'Mystery outings are always exciting,' she said carefully, genuinely excited.

His unexpected grin was lazily amused, setting her cheeks on fire again as he strolled towards her and ushered her out of the door.

Seconds later they were standing at the edge of the path, waiting for the traffic to clear before crossing the road. There was a brief break in the traffic but his sudden grip held her back when normally she'd have run, dodging the motorcycle in the outside lane.

Tom clicked his tongue, his hand tight as a vice on her arm. 'Hasn't anybody ever taught you how to cross the road safely?' he chided, not letting her go until the lights at the end of the road changed—leaving such an enormous gap that a herd of turtles could have crossed safely. 'Losing a casualty officer would be inconvenient for the rest of us.'

Peevishly she suggested that he think about that next time he threatened her with the sack.

'Your job's not in danger at this minute,' he said easily. 'Right now I couldn't face the paperwork.'

Ten minutes later they were heading away from the hospital, inching past Lord's cricket ground—the traffic horrendous. 'Friday night,' Tom reminded her, after it took two traffic light changes before there was space for them to cross an intersection. 'They're all rushing to get out of London for the weekend.'

She was impressed by the fluid ease with which he patiently manoeuvred the big car through the chaos, vastly different to the jerky stop-start way she drove herself. 'Are you happy to be back in London?'

'I would have preferred to return to Oxford,' he admitted. 'But this post was too good to turn down.'

'Where were you based in the States?'

'Boston.' He didn't seem surprised that she knew he'd been away. 'Been there?'

She shook her head. 'I did my elective in vascular surgery at Seattle under the supervision of one of Jeremy's friends from med school, Isobel Newman.'

'You're interested in surgery?'

She stiffened. 'Is that so strange?'

They were turning left into a narrow tree-lined street, and once the car straightened out he glanced across at her again. 'I'm surprised you worked with Isobel. I wouldn't have thought you two compatible.'

Poppy had forgotten that he'd know Isobel but, of course, as one of Jeremy's classmates she'd obviously been in Tom's year as well. 'We got on very well,' she said tightly, realising that he'd sidestepped her question about her doing surgery.

But Tom seemed relaxed again. 'That must mean you didn't tell her any of your alien stories. She wouldn't have tolerated any nonsense.'

The fact that, despite her relative youth, her supervisor had been extremely strait-laced and at times bewildered by the haze of confusion that sometimes surrounded Poppy, didn't mean that they hadn't been compatible. Poppy had pulled her weight, worked hard and had learned a great deal from the attachment. 'I'd appreciate it if you stopped harping on about aliens,' she said chillingly. 'It's become boring.'

He gave her a heart-thudding grin as he

pulled the car up to a tall white fence. 'You'd rather I commented on your make-up skills?' he asked softly.

She flushed, a hot deep red. 'Talk about aliens all you want,' she choked. 'I love it.'

'Sorry.' He'd released his seat belt but instead of opening his door he lifted one finger and tapped her freckled nose, his eyes veiled but disturbingly gentle—so disturbingly gentle that Poppy felt all the moisture in her mouth evaporate. 'You didn't look so bad,' he said quietly. 'Like a young child dressing up. I rather liked it.'

'Let's get back to the aliens,' she snarled.

He smiled, an easy, wonderful smile. Then, before she could get her thoughts together enough to ask where they were, he was out of the car and opening the large gates in front of them. He parked the car in a garage at the end of the drive, opened her door and ushered her into the brick house beside it. 'Come on,' he said smoothly, 'let's get you inside.'

And then what? She looked at him nervously but his enigmatic expression wasn't giving anything away.

CHAPTER SIX

'THIS is yours?' Poppy twirled in the spacious entrance hall, unbuttoning her coat while Tom disengaged the burglar alarm that had started bleeping as soon as they'd entered. 'Goodness!'

Tom hung her coat on a tall wooden stand near the door. 'Find the kitchen and choose some wine.' He headed for the broad staircase at the far end of the hall. 'I won't be long.'

Poppy spent a few minutes admiring the huge, sparsely furnished open living area, a fern-filled conservatory and, she decided—pressing her nose to the conservatory glass and squinting into the darkness—an enormous garden that stretched down to a canal.

'Kitchen,' she told herself firmly, dragging herself away from the plants. Off the living room she found the most impressive kitchen she'd ever seen. Like something out of a magazine, it was all gleaming white and steel, hanging copper and cast-iron pans, broad expanses of spotless benches, double sinks and ovens.

It wasn't the sort of kitchen where a person

would feel comfortable making instant pot
noodles.

Curiously she pulled open the fridge, only
remembering his suggestion that she choose
some wine when she saw several bottles lying
inside the well-stocked interior. Frowning, she
studied the labels. She could have a French
white Burgundy, an Australian Chardonnay or
a New Zealand sauvignon blanc.

Poppy sucked in her cheeks. One of her aunts
had recently been bungy-jumping in New
Zealand so that seemed as good a choice as
any. She left the bottle on a bench while she
wandered around, opening immaculately
orderly cupboards and drawers at random—
enjoying the secret look into Tom's life.

'Having fun?'

His quiet words made her jump. 'S-searching
for the opener,' she said nervously, trying not
to stare too obviously when he crouched at a
cupboard and the faded denim jeans he now
wore tightened revealingly. The cupboard, she
saw, housed a modest collection of wines.

'Down here.' He lifted out an opener, then
reached for the bottle she'd left on the bench,
his mouth lifting appreciatively as he studied
her choice. 'You're a connoisseur. This is one
of my best bottles.' He'd changed into an open-
necked blue shirt and rolled up the sleeves, and

as he uncorked the wine she could see the muscles in his arms working. In casual clothes he looked younger, more approachable, devastating.

'I know what I like,' she said evasively.

He lifted two gleaming glasses from yet another pristine cupboard, poured the wine and handed her one glass. 'Cheers.'

'World peace.' She took a mouthful, grimacing involuntarily at the sudden bite of sharp sourness she hadn't been expecting. Thankfully Tom didn't see the gesture as his thoughtful gaze was on his own wine.

'Wonderful, isn't it?'

'Startling,' she said brightly. 'Fresh. Fruity.' Lip-shrinkingly sour. But, worried that not drinking the wine would make her seem even more immature than he already thought her, she took another sip.

'Now business.' Azure-midnight eyes looked directly at her, very serious now. 'The other room's more comfortable.'

Poppy paled. This was it. Stiffly, she walked ahead of him through the arch into the living room. She perched on the edge of a wide armchair, part of an L-shaped arrangement of two chairs and a low couch at one end of the room around an open fire that he must have lit before coming into the kitchen. She took another sip of her wine and stared fixedly into the flames.

She felt him sit at the end of the couch beside her and out of the corner of her eye saw him balance the ankle of one trainer-clad foot on his opposite knee, the knee that rested inches from hers.

The best defence, Poppy decided, was confrontation. 'I'm sorry about what I said to Lucy,' she said quickly. 'I. . .I was preoccupied and I didn't realise what I was saying. On Monday I'll make sure she understands that it was all my fault, and nothing like this will ever happen again. Ever.'

She took a quick mouthful of the wine, relieved to find that it tasted better. 'Something I should have said a lot earlier is that I'm very, very sorry about telling everyone what happened that night at St John's. I behaved abominably and. . .well, I should never have been there in the first place and—' she was flushing now '—I certainly should have kept my mouth shut.'

'None of us behaved particularly thoughtfully that night,' he said flatly. 'You were the least at fault.'

'She. . .she was very beautiful.'

'Yes.' He was watching her steadily now.

'I suppose,' Poppy faltered. 'I suppose you must have been in love with her.'

'Do you?' He took a long swallow of his wine. 'That's an interesting supposition.'

One he hadn't denied. 'You're not a dishonourable man,' she said huskily. 'I can't imagine you. . . If Adele really loved her husband she'd never have been with you. I mean she might have thought about it but she wouldn't actually have. . .' But she stopped there and briefly lifted anxious eyes to enigmatic blue ones, before sliding them back to the fire—deciding that that didn't seem the wisest course to pursue. 'I mean—'

'I get your point. Enjoying your wine?'

'Yes.' She sipped it distractedly. 'And if you both loved each other—'

'Look, we'd been to a staff dinner, that's all,' Tom said wearily. 'Adele only came back to pick up some notes I'd promised her and she. . .' He hesitated. 'She'd just discovered that Jackson was having an affair with his secretary,' he added finally. 'She wasn't acting normally.'

'You. . .you mean you weren't already involved—?'

'She was hurt and she was angry and she'd been drinking. For a few minutes she considered hurting her husband in return.' He grimaced. 'Seeing you in my bed changed her mind about that.'

Poppy sucked in her cheeks. 'She thought you and I were. . .?'

'That would be the natural assumption,' he said in a deep voice. 'Poppy, you were quite naked.'

'Yes, but—' she couldn't even look at him '—surely she didn't think—'

'It hardly mattered.' He lifted one broad shoulder. 'Just heightened the irony when Jackson found out what had happened and all hell broke loose.'

'Oh.' She hung her head, wondering what Tom had done to comfort her then. Despite his assurance about Adele's motives, the nurse had been furious about seeing Poppy there and Poppy wondered if her intentions had been less straightforward than he'd thought. 'Adele. . .?'

'Is happily remarried,' he said briefly. 'She had her third child last Christmas.'

Oh. So they kept in touch. 'And Mr Jackson?'

'Married his secretary.' There was a long silence and he finished his wine and leaned forward to top up both their glasses.

'I'm sorry you had to leave Britain,' she said quietly. 'With the scandal and everything. Surely, if you'd explained—'

'I'd already been accepted for Boston. Leaving Britain six months earlier than I'd intended wasn't especially inconvenient.'

And let him protect Adele's pride, too, Poppy noted forlornly. She took more of the cool wine. 'If it hadn't been for me, Adele and you might—'

'Poppy?'

'Mmm?'

'Enough.'

Oh. Enough. Fine. Poppy watched the fire. 'From now on,' she promised, 'you'll have no complaints about my behaviour. 'You've told me off and I've learned my lesson.'

'I don't believe I actually got as far as *telling you off*,' he said dryly, 'although that was my intention.'

'And now everything's settled,' she continued, ignoring that. 'I feel cleansed,' she mused. 'That's it. Spiritually cleansed.'

Seeing the way he lifted his eyes to the ceiling might have pricked her bubble, had her confidence not been so boosted by getting all the horrible business over with so efficiently. She tipped her head back. 'So,' she said lightly, tilting her head back to gaze around the room which—apart from the suite they were sitting on and a rather beautiful wooden table and matching set of chairs—was almost empty, 'where's the rest of the furniture?'

He tilted his head, studying her. 'Yet to be bought,' he said finally, just when she'd decided that he was going to ignore the question. 'I've only had this place three months.'

'Jeremy's just moved house too. He's bought on the river.'

'Really?' Tom looked surprised. 'So he's finally decided to stay in Oxford?'

For the next little while they talked about Jeremy and Oxford and her parents, and by the time she finished her second glass of wine Poppy was completely relaxed, bewildered about why she'd ever been worried about this conversation at all.

'You know this really is *very* good,' she said happily, lifting her glass as she drained the final drop. 'Wonderful stuff.'

'Sorry.' He shook the empty bottle. 'That's the end of it.' He eased himself up. 'My choice next?'

'Be my guess,' she said expansively. 'Oops.' She giggled. 'I mean, guest.'

He sighed as he retrieved her glass. 'Fruit juice, I think. And food.'

'No food.' Although her stomach promptly grumbled and she remembered that she'd been too busy for lunch she protested, enjoying talking with him too much to want him to leave. She shook her head, but that was a mistake because immediately the room moved and she clutched the side of her head. 'Oh, dear.' Surely she couldn't be tipsy? Surely not after two glasses?

'Yes, food.' He was at the archway. 'I've been meaning to offer you a proper dinner all week,' he said, surprising her into befuddled silence, for never in a thousand years would she have guessed that. 'You looked so frail and wan that first morning when you fainted, and when you scoffed that toast I realised that you probably still lived on instant pot noodles.'

'Along with sandwiches and junk food,' she admitted sheepishly. 'Plus McDonald's now.'

'Given that the only alternative is the hospital canteen, that's hardly surprising.' He was speaking from the kitchen and a short time later he brought her a glass of orange juice. 'Stay by the fire.'

But a few minutes later she found herself following him.

She stumbled across the stool she'd meant to sit on and he caught her and steered her onto it. 'How much do you normally drink?' he asked suspiciously.

Poppy gazed up at him, peering into his eyes. He really was the most attractive man she'd ever seen and his eyes were quite, quite exquisite. 'Possibly not enough,' she conceded.

'How much?'

She concentrated. Since that dreadful night

at St John's, very, very little. 'A glass at Christmas.'

He swore, then swivelled her stool so that she was propped in the corner. 'Stay there,' he instructed firmly, jerking his head away when she tried to touch his mouth. 'Don't move.'

'Yes, sir. Boss.' She flicked a few loosened ringlets back over her shoulder. 'It's ironic, isn't it?'

He frowned. 'What?'

'Life.'

He muttered something uncharitable under his breath, before returning to chopping up whatever he'd been chopping up.

But Poppy wasn't offended. 'I'm not tipsy,' she said carefully. 'I don't drink.'

Tom lifted his eyes briefly to the ceiling but merely said, 'Tell me more about Jeremy. Still playing rugby?'

And so she burbled on for the time it took him to prepare dinner. He told her to stay still while he carried everything through into the living room, and when it was time for her to go too he took her arm.

'I'm perfectly capable of walking,' she said indignantly, although not too indignantly because she liked him holding her.

'Just sit.' He folded her into the seat. 'Eat.'

The food, for Poppy, was a revelation. 'This

is fantastic,' she said earnestly, chomping away on something red and delicious that he'd mixed with grilled pieces of chicken and red peppers and other odd-looking things. 'You know you could be a cook.'

'High praise,' he said lightly. 'You mean it's better than noodles?'

'Much.' She held up another one of the red things on the end of the fork. 'What exactly is this?'

'Poppy, where've you been?' he asked with a sigh. 'It's just a tomato. Sun-dried.'

She pointed to a green leaf. 'And this?'

'Basil.'

'Oh.' She kept eating until her plate was cleared. 'That was delicious.'

'And easy.' He frowned at her. 'You know you could make it.'

'No, I couldn't.' She shook her head firmly. 'Everything burns. I forget things.' Then she gave him another happy smile. 'You know, Tom, you have the nicest mouth—'

He grabbed her finger before it reached him, forcing it back to the table. 'Coffee,' he said abruptly, standing up and taking the mouth that held her attention out of her reach. 'I'll make coffee.'

When he reappeared a few minutes later, carrying a laden tray, she waved at him from

the luxurious depths of the couch. 'Here,' she
called. 'By the fire.'

But instead of sharing the couch he took the
armchair she'd sat in earlier. 'Milk or sugar?'

She shook her head, beaming at him as he
handed her a cup. 'You make the best coffee
in the world.'

'You haven't tasted it yet,' he said dryly.

'But I remember from St John's,' she
insisted. Her eyes focused on the tiny creases in
his lower lip. 'And you have a great mouth——'

'Poppy, drink your drink.' All the tiny
creases flattened as his mouth tightened.

Obediently she drank some of the rich liquid,
then her attention swung back to his wonderful
mouth. 'I bet you're a fantastic kisser.'

His face turned wary. 'Poppy——' he began
warningly, but she hadn't finished.

'I bet you turn women's legs weak,' she continued. 'Adele Jackson looked pretty impressed.
I bet her legs were weak. I bet she——'

'I bet you're still drunk,' he muttered. 'Two
glasses of wine—who the hell would believe
it?' He eased the cup from her grip and replaced
it on the tray. 'Up you get. Home time.'

She uncurled her legs and let him pull her
up, stepping delicately into the shoes she'd discarded earlier—all the while clutching onto his

hands while she pouted up at him. 'It's my breasts, isn't it?'

He blinked. 'What?'

'My breasts,' she said brightly, tugging her fingers free so that she could show him what she meant. 'They're too small.'

When her hands lowered to the hem of her sweatshirt and started to tug it up he grabbed them. 'That's enough,' he said tightly. Before she could even catch her breath he twirled her around, steered her towards the door and threaded her arms through her coat sleeves.

Poppy tilted her head back and smiled at him. 'How about silicone?'

He swore under his breath, reaching for the buttons of her coat and not stopping till she was buttoned from chin to knee. 'Why the hell didn't you tell me you're teetotal?' he muttered, pulling on his own jacket.

'I'm not,' she lied. 'Look, I know you like big breasts—'

'Stop! Stop right now!' Grimly he shoved her out of the door onto the porch.

'I suppose silicone might make them might feel a bit hard,' she said doubtfully, poking one breast experimentally through her coat. 'But—'

The clamp of a big hand over her mouth smothered the rest of the words. Impossibly dark blue eyes glared down at her. 'Poppy,' he

grated, 'shut up. If you don't I will strangle
you. Understand?'

Mutely she nodded. He was magnificent
when he was angry.

Tentatively the hand loosened then, apparently deciding that his threat had achieved what
he'd intended, he took it away. 'Get in the
car.'

Obediently she trotted into the garage and
climbed inside the car while he saw to the gates.
He shot her a brief, hard look before backing
the car out, a look she met with a bright smile
for she was imagining herself with enormous
breasts. He wouldn't be able to resist her, she
decided. She'd ask for the biggest size they did.

The drive back to her flat seemed to take
mere seconds. To her delight he escorted her
all the way to her door, lifting the key
impatiently out of her hands as she fumbled
with the lock.

He opened the door, bundled her inside,
walked quickly and imperiously around the flat
but then walked out, shutting the door very
firmly on her wave of effusive thanks and offers
of tea.

Disappointed but not dejected, Poppy leaned
back against the door, listening to him
descending the stairs and wondering whether a

first-year SHO could really afford breast enlargement surgery.

On Monday morning Poppy slunk into Casualty like a worried stoat. From some deep reserve that had gone untapped all weekend she managed to muster a smile for her colleague who, as usual before his shift, was sitting in the common-room studying. Unfortunately her suggestion that she stayed in minors all week did not win instant approval.

'I do prefer majors,' Derek admitted, 'but Tom's the one who decides where we cover. Talk to him.'

But talking to Tom didn't suit Poppy at all. 'How about just today, then? Don't wait for him to say anything, just take over majors.'

Derek shrugged. 'OK.'

'Thanks.' That at least should make it easy for her to keep a low profile today. A fraction happier, she pulled on her white coat and went looking for Lucy.

But the sister cut off her carefully rehearsed apology with a smile, explaining that she'd already told everyone that the story about Tom had all been a practical joke. 'Think no more about it,' she said lightly. 'I should have had enough sense to know you already knew each other—I'd forgotten his reaction when he first saw your name on the intake list.'

'Um. . . H-how exactly did he react?' Poppy tried not to look too interested.

Lucy obviously saw through her because she laughed. '"Thoughtfully" is probably the closest I can come,' she said cheerfully.

Thoughtfully? Poppy blanched. He'd probably been thinking about resigning. 'I'm going to be very careful about what I say in future,' she said.

'Not too careful.' Lucy laughed again. 'The look on Tom's face on Friday when he realised why we'd all been fussing over him was worth all the trouble.'

Poppy sucked in her cheeks. 'It was rather funny.'

'It was hilarious.' Lucy took her arm and steered her out of the office. 'And I won't say a word about the two of you. I promise.'

Poppy's mouth dropped open. 'Oh, but—'

'You're exactly what he needs,' the sister advised. 'He's too used to women falling all over him.'

'But we're not—'

'Of course you're not.' But, to Poppy's alarm, Lucy's smile was warmly knowing. 'I won't tell a soul.'

Oh, dear. As Lucy turned into majors Poppy

veered off towards minors, chewing her lower lip worriedly.

'Monday morning's always the worst,' the triage nurse told her a while later when she had a few seconds to catch her thoughts amongst the deluge of patients. 'All the things people have stored up all weekend.'

Along with the normal catalogue of minor injuries, she had to deal with several patients with forearm fractures, giving her more practice at the techniques Tom had taught her the week before. By the third patient she was feeling very confident—it was exhilarating, considering that before starting the attachment she'd barely have known where to start.

Shortly after noon, by which time the department had quietened considerably, she saw someone whom she suspected had fractured a scaphoid bone, a small wrist bone. Left untreated, the bone could lose its blood supply, leading—amongst other problems—to long-term stiffness and pain.

'I can't actually see a fracture on any of the X-rays,' Poppy told her patient, Mrs Burton. Once more she probed her swollen wrist to confirm that the major tenderness was in a little pocket near her thumb, referred to as the 'anatomical snuffbox'. 'But not all breaks are immediately obvious on an X-ray.'

After explaining the reasons for being especially cautious with this sort of injury, and with the skilled assistance of one of the plaster nurses guiding her—for this was the first time Poppy had handled this fracture—she encased the arm in a below-elbow plaster that extended lower down the thumb than the normal plaster used for lower arm breaks.

While they waited for the warm plaster to harden, before fitting a sling, Poppy told Mrs Burton that she needed to attend the fracture clinic the next day so that the orthopaedic team could review her injury.

She heard the doors behind her swing open and shut but, assuming that it was someone looking for supplies, didn't bother to turn around. 'They'll repeat the X-ray in ten days or so to see if a fracture's visible, before deciding whether to remove the plaster.'

'What's this?' Tom's deep voice made her jump as he leaned over her shoulder. 'Scaphoid?'

'Clinically, not radiologically,' Poppy said in a brittle voice, her whole body suddenly hot and stiff. Three days ago she'd gone to his home, drunk herself silly and tried to expose herself—and now he was here. Beside her. Looking as if nothing untoward had ever happened. 'But to be safe—'

'How did it happen?'

'I fell like this, Doctor,' said Mrs Burton, holding her non-injured arm outstretched, palm bent back, 'off a step.'

Tom glanced at the films on the board. 'Lunate all right? Median nerve? Radial styloid?'

'Fine.' Too embarrassed to face him, Poppy kept her eyes on her notes but she sensed him walking to the X-ray board.

'Good,' he said finally. 'The films look normal but you're wise to be cautious.'

Poppy smiled tensely at Mrs Burton and the plaster nurse who was busy fitting a sling, trying to pretend that he wasn't there. 'Come back if you've any worries,' she told her patient, passing her a photocopied list of the potential problems that could occur with the plaster. 'Take care.' Then—hurriedly—she left the room.

There was just one patient waiting to see her, a young man who'd twisted his ankle and who took only a few minutes to examine before one of the staff nurses took over, fitting his ankle with a Tubigrip bandage.

When she emerged from the cubicle Tom was leaning against one of the desks in minors, waiting for her—his arms folded and his hard face unreadable.

Poppy felt her stomach drop the way it did in high-speed lifts. Why on earth did people say that alcohol dulled memories? She could remember every excruciating moment of Friday night. 'Th-thank you for checking those X-rays,' she said nervously.

'Scaphoid fractures can be difficult,' he acknowledged, his eyes holding her fluttering gaze.

She shifted her feet. 'If there's still nothing to see in ten days, will the orthopods just remove the plaster?'

'Unless there's persistent pain, in which case an isotope scan is indicated. A fracture would show up as a hot spot on the films.'

'Oh.' Poppy hadn't known that. Her hands were trembling and she put them behind her back. 'Er. . .should I have asked for a scan today?'

'No.'

'Oh.' He was still watching her and she felt her face flushing. How on earth could she have mentioned silicone implants? 'Too soon, I suppose, on the scan for anything to show.'

He nodded curtly. 'Correct.'

Poppy could stand the tension no longer. It was obvious that he was waiting for her to say something about Friday night. 'Tom, I'm sorry,' she blurted. 'About everything. I should never have accepted the wine—'

'Shut up, Poppy,' he said wearily. 'I don't care about Friday. For God's sake, no more apologies. I can't stand it.'

Subdued, she muttered, 'Yes, Tom.'

'Consider it forgotten.'

'Yes, Tom.' If only.

'What I want to discuss is your duty swap with Derek,' he said, the astuteness of the gaze that probed her own suggesting that he knew exactly why she'd wanted to avoid majors this morning. 'The rosters are arranged to optimise training and they're not to be altered without discussion with me.'

'No, Tom.'

'If it's still quiet here this afternoon I want you to give Derek a hand next door.'

'Yes, Tom.'

He checked his watch. 'Go and have lunch now while there's nobody waiting. I'll cover.'

'Yes, Tom.' She suppressed the urge to ask him what she should eat and turned away meekly, pleased for once with the way she'd handled herself. 'Your problem is you usually talk too much,' she told herself as she hurried along the corridor. 'Keep your mouth shut and you'll be all right.'

After lunch there wasn't anybody waiting in

minors and so she spent the afternoon moving
between majors and minors, depending on
where she was required. To her relief, Tom
wasn't there and Lucy told her that he was running a clinic in another part of the hospital.

Majors was chaotic although, thankfully,
most of the beds held patients who'd been
referred by GPs directly to the relevant hospital
team so neither Derek nor Poppy had to see
them.

Of the cases that did come straight to
Casualty, it was very much a medical afternoon,
Most of the patients she had to refer presented
with medical problems, including two with
heart attacks and two with strokes.

The on-call medical registrar's face was
strained as he looked up from the notes he was
scribbling and accepted her fifth referral of the
afternoon, a middle-aged woman with right
lower lobe pneumonia.

'I've taken all the bloods, gases, X-rays, put
in a Venflon and sent sputum to Micro,' she
told him, knowing how busy he'd been. 'If you
tell me which antibiotics you want we'll give
the first dose down here.'

'Thanks, that'll be a big help. I'll take a look
at her.' Some of the strain lessened. 'Derek's
given us three more patients as well, and there
are at least five GP referrals still waiting. My

SHO's off sick and the locum who was supposed to be here by five hasn't arrived. I've a
brand new houseman fresh out of medical
school, who's still struggling with the admissions that arrived before lunch, *and* I'm
supposed to be in clinic.'

Poppy smiled sympathetically. 'I'll write up
the admission for you.'

He managed a weary smile. 'You're a tro-
uper. Would you have a minute to pop a
Venflon into the chap with the left hemiparesis
so the nurses can start his fluids?'

'Sure.' Once she'd finished that Poppy
checked her watch. The day had whizzed past.
Her shift had officially finished fifteen minutes
ago and, short of handing over to the new
casualty officers and writing up the admission
she'd just promised, she had nothing else to do.

Returning to the common-room soon after,
she realised that the evening stretched bleakly
ahead of her. Unenthusiastic about another
fraught night alone, brooding over the fool
she'd made of herself on Friday night, Poppy
checked the notice-board as she shrugged out
of her white coat. Her eyes narrowed on a list
of lectures offered every Monday evening by
the post-graduate society. Tonight's lecture was
called 'Trends in US Trauma Management—
Lessons for Britain?' The speaker was Tom.

'The room will be dark,' she said speculatively. 'He'll never see me.' And the notice said that refreshments were supplied. 'How can you turn down free sandwiches?'

Easily, it turned out, for when she arrived—*deliberately* late for once because she hoped that would guarantee lowered lights and no trouble slipping discreetly into the back of the hall—the generous pile of sandwiches on a trolley outside the lecture theatre was barely touched. Wrinkling her nose, Poppy realised why. Sardines in tomato paste, egg with sausage, and chocolate spread were the only choices, all white bread, all dry and none of them remotely appealing—presumably a sample of the dreaded hospital canteen's merchandise.

Electing to grab a Big Mac later, she eased open the lecture-hall door and peered inside. To her dismay, the door opened at the floor of the theatre a few yards from where Tom stood at a lectern, talking to the assembled crowd.

He saw her instantly, of course, and stopped talking, his brows lifting mockingly as she hesitated, torn between coming in and running out but knowing that whatever she did she'd already made a fool of herself. 'Don't be shy,' he said dryly, earning a chuckle from his audience. 'None of us bite. Seats down the front.'

CHAPTER SEVEN

BLUSHING furiously, Poppy dashed towards the first row of seats that still had spare room, well aware that she had the attention of the entire hall. Once seated she sent him a resentful glare, a resentment that sharpened when two other doctors walked in after her and he barely glanced their way.

'Within fourteen minutes of the paramedic crew arriving at the scene this man was in the emergency room,' Tom said, flicking up slides of a young man with multiple shotgun wounds. 'Within eleven minutes of arrival he'd been evaluated, intubated, transfusion had begun and he was in the operating theatre. Time from injury to surgery thirty-six minutes, well within the so-called golden hour for resuscitation. These times are good, but not exceptional.'

Poppy didn't have any difficulty concentrating on the lecture for, although her eyes showed an unhealthy tendency to linger on him rather than his slides, the talk was interesting, good-humoured and witty.

Clearly he loved his work and judging from the rush of questions from his audience at the

end Poppy wasn't the only one infected by his
enthusiasm.

'Do you envisage facilities such as these
becoming more widely available in Britain?'
someone asked.

'High quality acute care like this is expensive.' Tom grimaced. 'We'd need the political
will to institute it. Currently we don't have that.'

A sleek, dark-haired woman who sat two
along from Poppy raised her hand. 'Yet you
chose to return to this country?'

'I'm an optimist,' Tom said evenly, exchanging an easy smile with the woman.

Poppy looked at her sharply, then frowned,
recognising her face but unable to pinpoint why.
She wondered which speciality allowed the
woman to stay so immaculately unruffled.

'And it helps to have an ideal to strive for,'
Tom continued. 'There are forty accidental
deaths a day in this country and accidents
remain the primary cause of lives lost under
age thirty-five. A network of first-class trauma
units would make a significant dent on those
figures.'

As she listened to him Poppy's enthusiasm
grew. Until now her precise plans for the future
had been hazy. She'd narrowed her choice down
to surgery but nothing more specific. Trauma
was a complicated speciality, involving long

training in practically every area—ideally including time abroad gaining experience—but his presentation was inspiring and when it finished she darted to the front to question him.

But he merely pushed a heavy sheaf of notes into her hands. 'At the door,' he told her. 'Quick.'

So she found herself dishing out sets of the printed notes to each doctor as the audience slowly drained out of the auditorium. When she turned back towards Tom the elegant woman who'd asked the question earlier was perched on the edge of the desk beside him, her gleaming hair in a neat chignon reminding Poppy of how untidy hers must be after a long day's work.

The woman wore a smart red suit that clung to her perfect figure, and her legs were crossed to reveal shapely calves and knees. She regarded Poppy coolly as she approached.

'There're some left,' Poppy said huskily, her eyes darting between the two of them, still not able to place the woman but uncomfortable about her easy familiarity with Tom.

The woman lifted the remaining papers from Poppy before she could pass them to him. 'I'll take them,' she said smoothly.

'Thanks, Poppy.' Tom was sorting his slides and sounded distracted.

'Poppy?' His companion frowned and she stared at Poppy's tense face. One beautifully manicured hand touched Tom's forearm. 'I know that name from somewhere.'

Tom's head came up sharply and his eyes spoke a warning to Poppy, a warning she didn't understand, but when he spoke his voice was calm. 'Poppy's one of my new cas officers. Poppy, meet Janet DeBeer. Janet's a consultant histopathologist here.'

Poppy smiled a hesitant acknowledgement but the other doctor was still frowning. 'You're not. . . Are you Jeremy Brown's kid sister?' she asked slowly. Her frown darkened and she looked sharply at Tom. 'From St John's?'

Poppy exchanged a quick panicky look with Tom, murmured something about being late and fled, appalled. She remembered where she knew the other doctor from now. She'd been a registrar with Tom at St John's. She probably knew everything.

'Coward,' she muttered, catching sight of her reflection as she dashed along the corridor and knowing that nothing on earth could have dragged her back to face that woman's scorn.

Poppy Brown, trauma surgeon in training, had her first setback the next day when she almost mistook her patient's fractured neck of femur for a soft tissue injury.

Tom saw her taking a second look at the X-ray and quietly pointed out the almost imperceptible overlap that showed an impacted fracture. 'Easy to miss,' he said briskly, 'particularly as she's still able to take weight on the limb.'

But Poppy squirmed. Knowing that a radiologist would have reported the fracture within twenty-four hours, allowing her to arrange for her patient to come back again, didn't make her feel any better about getting the diagnosis wrong. 'I'm normally quite sharp with X-rays,' she said huskily, 'but clearly not as good as I thought.'

He looked irritated. 'Your expectations of yourself are too high. None of us is perfect and you're still only a junior SHO.'

Poppy swallowed. It wasn't true that nobody was perfect. From where she was standing, he looked pretty much as perfect as it was possible to be. 'Tom, about last night...' she said, allowing the words to trail away.

'Janet won't say anything so you can stop fretting.' His mouth compressed. 'She has the gift of discretion,' he added pointedly.

Unlike her. The words went unspoken, but understood, and Poppy walked away miserably.

* * *

Late that afternoon Lucy called to her from Resusc. 'Poppy, here, please.'

Two patients were already in the unit: one, judging from his cardiac trace, with an infarct, being seen by a medical registrar; the other, a middle-aged man vomiting blood who Tom was dealing with. He met her eyes briefly when she walked in, then returned immediately to his patient.

Lucy beckoned her to the empty bed. 'Unknown adult male in respiratory distress via the ambulance service one minute,' she said, pulling a resuscitation trolley closer to the head of the bed. 'Make that ten seconds,' she said, tilting her head as a siren sounded close by and hurrying to open the doors that opened into the ambulance bay.

Poppy pulled on a pair of gloves then snapped open the emergency drug box and tore the plastic coverings from a large Venflon in preparation for insertion.

She and Lucy exchanged grim looks when the man was wheeled in—sitting bolt upright on the stretcher, heaving for breath, eyes dropping shut, his colour a dreadful blue-grey. 'Ray Powers, you never learn,' muttered Lucy as they transferred him onto the casualty trolley.

'Found collapsed in Regent's Park,' said the

tallest of the two ambulance officers. 'No identification. Unable to give history. Respirations forty but weakening. Cardiac rhythm sinus and stable. No response to two point five milligrams nebulised salbutamol. We've only given him twenty-four per cent oxygen since he looked like chronic airways disease.'

'We know him,' Poppy replied. 'You did the right thing.'

While Lucy removed Mr Powers's grubby shirt and connected him to a cardiac monitor Poppy lifted the oxygen mask and swapped it for a hospital mask already primed with nebuliser solution. She grimaced when, despite his distress, he resisted, gritting his teeth and shaking his head as she tried to suction around his mouth—clawing weakly at her hands, despite Lucy's best efforts to hold him still. 'I'm only trying to help,' she said clearly, murmuring approval when he dropped his arms. 'Let me help.'

She listened to his chest, then started the nebuliser. While Lucy held his arm she inserted the Venflon she'd prepared into a vein in his forearm, before withdrawing some blood and injecting a dose of hydrocortisone. 'I need an aminophylline infusion. Two-fifty milligrams in two-fifty millilitres over five hours. No bolus.' It was likely that he hadn't been taking his medication but it was important to wait for a blood assay to be sure before giving more of the drug because an overdose could cause fatal arrhythmia.

Lucy nodded. 'Pulse one-twelve,' she said quickly, snapping open several ampoules of the drugs while Poppy probed his brachial artery in preparation for taking a blood gas sample. 'BP one hundred over seventy. Twenty millimetres of paradoxus. Radiographer on her way.'

'Mr Powers, one more needle,' Poppy warned, smiling her thanks to Lucy as she took hold of his elbow. 'Last one.' She popped the needle beneath the skin and then into the artery, feeling a satisfying pop as it punctured the wall and began filling the syringe. As soon as she'd withdrawn the needle another nurse, signalled by Lucy, covered the site with a wad of cotton wool, holding it firmly.

By the time the results came back Reception had located all his notes and Poppy grimaced at the blood gas measurements. He was in respiratory failure, low on oxygen but also retaining high levels of carbon dioxide—results considerably worse than the last time he'd required ventilation.

And so far the drugs had had little effect. He was clearly more tired, the effort of breathing exhausting him into near stupor. The chest

X-ray wasn't especially different from one taken six months earlier, but there was a minor increase in shadowing at the right base which could indicate infection.

By now Tom had taken his patient up to Theatre and the medical registrar who'd been seeing the patient in the next bed had gone as well.

'Coronary care,' Lucy told her, passing her the phone so that she could bleep him back.

'He's tiring,' she said, after explaining everything to the registrar when he answered. 'He needs ventilation.'

But the registrar apparently knew Mr Powers and when he returned to examine him he shook his head doubtfully. 'We won't be able to wean him off the machine,' he mused. 'We had loads of trouble last time and his gases were better then. Plus we haven't a spare bed so we'd have to shunt someone else out of ICU. Mr Powers has been deteriorating badly this year—I think this is his limit.'

Poppy frowned, certain that ventilation was his only hope. 'There's no one you can move?'

'There is one,' he admitted. 'A man in cardiogenic shock we could probably switch to CCU, but this chap's not a good candidate for ventilation anyway.'

'But he's asthmatic as well so some of his

disease is reversible,' she said urgently, 'and if infection's contributing then once he's over that he'll improve.'

He tapped the shadowing. 'If it looked significant I might agree,' he countered. 'But this isn't enough to make much difference and, besides, he's afebrile and his white count's barely elevated.'

'But he's only fifty-eight,' she protested. 'You can't just let him die.'

'I'm not saying that.' He frowned at her. 'We'll put him on the ward—full treatment, physio, experiment with antibiotics and oxygen—and see how he gets on.'

'Doxapram?'

He lifted one shoulder. 'We'll see.'

She looked tensely back through the doors into Resusc. 'He won't last on his own. He's virtually comatose now.'

He sighed. 'If it's so important to you ask the ICU SR,' he said finally. 'If she agrees to take him then, fine, we'll take our cardiac chap out and admit him there.'

Poppy smiled, relief washing over her like a wave. 'Thanks. That's terrific.'

But her relief didn't last for although the ICU senior registrar came to see Mr Powers, short of advising on his oxygen needs, she refused to accept him into her unit. 'Long standing deteriorating respiratory failure,' she recited. 'CO2 retainer, past difficulties in weaning, no prospect of improvement.' She shrugged. 'Sorry but no. No bed.'

So, instead of going off to ICU where Poppy was convinced he needed to be, Mr Powers was taken to one of the acute medical beds. 'He won't make it,' she told Lucy angrily over the cup of tea the sister insisted that she stop for. 'He won't last more than a few hours.'

Lucy looked up but it wasn't until she left the room with a kind smile that Poppy realised that Tom was there. 'I heard,' he said when she opened her mouth. 'Hard not to overhear you fighting with John. He's a solid, gifted registrar, Poppy. Learn from him.'

'We weren't fighting,' she protested. 'I just don't understand why they won't give him a chance.'

Tom took the seat Lucy had vacated. 'Being an idealist in this job means you're in for a few knocks. The world doesn't read like a textbook.'

'I know that,' she said tightly. 'But he's been in the unit several times and made it out. Why not again?'

'Because he's dying.'

She caught her breath. 'If I'd managed to make him stay last week—'

'This isn't about you,' he said flatly.

But it was. It was completely about her. 'If he'd stayed last week he wouldn't be so ill now.'

'Perhaps not so quickly,' he acknowledged brutally. 'You may have gained him a few weeks but we're talking about end-stage respiratory failure. We can't cure him. You're not responsible for the condition of his lungs.'

She stared down at her hands, clasping them and unclasping them in her lap. 'You think I'm being ridiculous.'

'I think you're young. As you become more experienced you'll discover there's a time when it's better to stand back.'

She looked up cynically. '"A surgeon's greatest gift is knowing when not to operate"?'

He inclined his head. 'I've recited that even to my own medical students,' he admitted wryly. 'You might consider it clichéd but it's true.'

Wearily Poppy checked her watch. It was after six. 'I'll go up and see him before I leave.'

'That's not a good idea.' Tom stopped her at the door, pushing it closed and leaning back on it to stop her leaving. 'Not tonight. He won't know you and even if he did he wouldn't want you there. You'll only get in the way and put the team on defensive.'

'Just to make sure—'

'No.' His eyes gleamed with determination. 'He's no longer your patient. Leave things alone.'

'I just want to say sorry,' she raged, angry at him, at the hospital and mostly at herself. 'I made a mistake last week and now he's going to die. Don't you understand that?'

'I understand you're trying to ease your own conscience. But that's not going to help him. Face your guilt and deal with it and you'll be a better doctor. Don't try and erase it the easy way by seeking absolution at his deathbed.'

She sank back on her heels and sucked in her cheeks. 'You're right,' she said dully, folding her arms around her. 'Of course you're right.'

There was a short silence, then he said abruptly, 'Let's get out of here,' startling her with the change of subject. 'I'll treat you to dinner.'

Poppy froze, unable to believe that after last time he wanted anything to do with her outside of business hours. 'I'm not dressed properly—'

'This isn't a date,' he said impatiently, promptly making her feel stupid because, of course, it wouldn't be. He was dating the lovely Janet, she reminded herself. Elegant and sophisticated with a huge bust, she added viciously.

Tom opened the door and shooed her ahead

of him. 'You worked through your lunch-break the same as I did so I assume you're just as hungry. Are you coming or not?'

Poppy swallowed. 'Yes.' Of course she was coming.

He took her to an Italian restaurant close to the hospital. At first their talk was carefully neutral—of Boston and Oxford, books and films—as if their earlier confrontation had drained them both, but when the waiter brought coffee after the meal she mentioned his lecture the night before. 'You inspired me,' she admitted with a self-conscious flush. 'I'm wondering about training in trauma.'

'You've organised a surgical rotation?'

She shook her head. 'I suppose I've always intended doing something surgical but I hadn't picked a field. Dad, being ENT, thinks that's a good career for a woman, and, of course, Jeremy's besotted with plastics, but part of the reason I applied for this casualty job was to give myself breathing place to sort out my own ideas.' She stirred her drink. 'The other part was that doing casualty here's a step towards joining the National's rotation afterwards.'

He frowned. 'Your name's not among the applicants for the next intake.'

Poppy's head snapped up. 'I haven't submitted my application yet. I didn't know you were on the selection panel.'

'As of this month I am.'

'Oh.' Embarrassed, she looked down. 'I'm sorry. I wasn't touting for a job.'

'I didn't think you were,' he said quietly, before finishing his coffee.

Poppy's pulse jumped nervously. He hadn't offered her any encouragement. As her consultant, it wouldn't have been unreasonable of him to do so. 'Do you think I'd be a suitable candidate?' she asked hesitantly.

'It's not an easy discipline.' He pushed his cup away and folded his arms, watching her warily. 'The training's demanding, competitive, exhausting. Doubly difficult as a woman if you intend to have a family—part-time training's still unrealistic and there'll always be younger graduates snapping at your heels and overtaking you in experience.'

She stiffened. 'But if a woman was fully committed. . .?'

Blue eyes narrowed assessingly. 'Are you?'

'I. . .think so.'

'"Think" isn't good enough,' he said flatly. 'What if you marry? Will your husband be flexible enough to follow you around the country, as well as abroad, for ten years? Will he be happy about you being on call half the week and spending hours on research and presentations and needing to work most weekends, and will you be prepared to be away from him for those hours? What if you get pregnant? Will your husband want to stay at home? If not, how will you feel about leaving your baby with child-minders while you work?'

'There's no husband yet,' she said stiffly, avoiding his gaze.

'Circumstances change.' He signalled for the bill. 'It's unfair and discriminatory but that's the reality for a woman in this field.'

In the car she said in a very small voice, 'So you don't recommend I apply?'

'I recommend you consider your options more fully,' he said evasively. 'Your family background is surgical. It would be easy to be swept up into the field without ever thinking properly about it.' He pulled the car into the hospital car park. 'Assess your interests and goals objectively. Perhaps your talents lie in another field?'

Apparently sensing her misery, he sighed as they crossed the road towards her flat. 'Poppy, don't look so downtrodden. I wanted to introduce a note of reality, not take away your enthusiasm.'

She trudged ahead of him up the stairs. 'Today has not been a good day,' she mumbled, then her mouth dropped open as she registered the smashed door to her flat. She stopped in the doorway, stunned, surveying the mess. 'It just got worse.'

Tom pushed ahead of her. 'Wait there,' he said grimly, striding into her bedroom and then towards the kitchen and the bathroom. 'What the hell were they looking for?'

'Drugs.' Poppy stepped gingerly into the main room. 'Hospital flat. Happens quite often. The neighbours warned me when I moved in.'

He swore. 'All your things. . .' His head snapped up at her sigh. 'What?'

She walked through the rubble, nudging the white foam that had once lined the couch. 'I haven't any things,' she said quietly. 'Only a suitcase of clothes and a few books.' She was feeling sorry for herself.

She crouched and retrieved a novel from the floor. The book was badly torn. 'But now, it seems, I have nothing.' Then, instead of crying, she found herself smiling. 'I'm a free spirit.'

Tom rolled his eyes. 'You're not free, you're hysterical,' he said matter-of-factly. 'It's the shock.' His eyes dropped to the book-cover she clutched. 'And your taste in literature, as always, is questionable.' He looked around. 'Where's the phone?'

'In the bedroom.' She spun around, her coat

flapping around her, feeling light and floaty. Although she knew that her reaction was odd, it seemed quite pleasant. If this was hysteria it wasn't that bad.

A few minutes later he reappeared. 'Security's coming,' he said briskly, apparently electing to ignore the way she was twirling through the chaos. 'Your suitcase is still here. Shall I pack some clothes?'

Poppy stopped, instantly becoming dizzy. She covered her eyes. 'Oh, dear.'

She heard him swear under his breath and then nothing. She opened her eyes again at a polite cough at the door. 'Mr Sweeny,' she said lightly. 'We meet again.'

'Sadly still no sign. . .er. . .of your suit,' the head of security said, although he didn't look particularly sad—almost chirpy, in fact. He looked around. 'Deary me, made a bit of a mess of it, then.'

'Never mind,' she said cheerfully. 'Could have been worse.'

'Sensible. . .er. . .attitude,' he said carefully, inspecting the wrecked couch. 'Third time this year, this place.'

Tom appeared from the bedroom, holding her suitcase and surveying the security man disapprovingly. 'Then isn't it about time security was improved?'

'Don't be so stuffy.' Poppy waved her hand at him. 'Mr Sweeny's been too busy searching for my suit.' She frowned at the suitcase. 'And where is that going?'

'With me,' he said tightly, collecting her arm as he marched past. 'You too.' He dragged the vaguely protesting Poppy towards the door. 'We'll leave you to it,' he said coolly. 'Doesn't look as if anything's missing.'

'Right you are, Mr. . .er. . . Grainger.' Mr Sweeny poked his foot thoughtfully at a piece of couch foam. 'We'll have this. . .er. . .sorted out in no time.'

Muttering something about hell freezing over, Tom tugged her downstairs.

'But my books,' she said. 'We've forgotten my books. Some of them looked undamaged.'

'They'll give you nightmares,' he said firmly, holding her arm to stop her skipping ahead of him at the road. 'You're better off without them.'

'Tom, I absolutely will not stay with you,' she said clearly as he drove her towards St John's Wood. 'You're very kind but I must refuse.'

He glanced in her direction, his mouth twitching. 'Really?'

'Really.' She nodded. 'Something's bound to go wrong. I'll set off the burglar alarms or break

things or set fire to something; I'll destroy your
beautiful kitchen.' It would be the end of this
fragile relationship they'd established. She
lifted her hands. 'Something disastrous will
happen.'

'I'm insured.' He drew up at the gates of his
home, then frowned. 'I'll increase my cover
tomorrow.' He opened his door. 'Poppy, believe
me, I'm not any happier about this than you are
but you're quite safe, you know.'

She knew that—trouble was she didn't really
want to be safe, and that was alarming. She
watched him open the gates, her eyes on the
easy strength of his movements, finding herself
imagining how it would feel to be his lover—
to be the gorgeous Janet, waiting in the car,
about to be taken to his bed and ravaged.

'Tonight, then,' she agreed when he returned
to the car. 'Tomorrow I'll find somewhere else
at the hospital.'

'You're not staying in another one of their
flats until Sweeny's upgraded security,' he said
firmly as he drove up the short tree-lined drive.
'They're not safe. Think of how Jeremy and
your parents would feel if I let you go back
there.'

Ah. Poppy sighed. So that was why he'd
insisted on bringing her here. 'I can look after
myself.'

'You're skin and bone,' he said scornfully. 'A child could knock you over, let alone a desperate drug addict.' He leaned across and opened her door, his arm briefly firm across her breasts, making her recoil against her seat. His eyes narrowed as he registered the movement and the flush that followed and she heard him sigh. 'Wait on the porch while I park in the garage.'

When they walked inside she sent him a baleful glare. 'I'm more than "skin and bone",' she said tightly. 'And I'd appreciate it if you refrained from comments about my appearance.'

He lowered her suitcase to the floor and she let him take her coat, tugging down the hem of her jumper when it rode up to reveal an inch of smooth midriff. 'You may prefer woman with big breasts,' she continued, 'but not all men do.'

'As I'm sure you know,' he said tightly.

'Yes.' Poppy sucked in her cheeks. Oh, dear. 'As I know.'

Tom tilted his head, watching her assessingly for a few taut minutes while she stood frozen, but when he finally spoke he said only, 'Tea before bed? Hot chocolate?'

'Tea, please.' She followed him through the living room and blinked when he bent to switch

on the fire, realising that it was an artificial pile
of logs and not the real thing. 'That's very
good,' she said faintly. 'I thought it was real.'

'It's supposed to be more eco-friendly,' he
said dryly, his tone suggesting he debated it.

Poppy settled herself on the couch, kicking
off her shoes so that she could curl her legs
beneath her. She tipped her head back against
the couch, wishing that this was real—wishing
that she was really here as his guest and not
just the leper to his good Samaritan.

'This is very kind of you.' She took the tea
when he brought it. 'I could have found somewhere else to stay.'

Tom sat on one of the chairs and crossed one
arm lazily behind his head. 'Let me guess,' he
said smoothly, watching her over the rim of his
cup as he took a sip of tea. 'One of your many
lovers?'

Poppy took a couple of hasty swallows of
her own tea and promptly scalded her tongue.
'S-something like that.'

'How does your family feel about this parade
of blond men through your life?'

'Obviously I don't. . .share every detail with
them,' she said stiltedly.

'Obviously.' His mouth twitched.

Averting her eyes for, relaxed and good-
humoured like this, he did crazy things to her

heart, she brushed some non-existent dust from the couch fabric. 'I'm not promiscuous,' she said carefully, regretting having given him any other impression. 'Not at all.'

'You're very wise.'

The words were heavy with amusement and she didn't dare look at him. 'In fact, I think sex should be a very special thing,' she added, 'between people with great. . .respect for one another.'

'Very sensible.'

'But I wouldn't want you to think I'm prudish,' she added hurriedly.

Tom choked on his tea. 'Prudish?' he rasped. 'Hardly.'

Oh. Poppy flushed, knowing exactly what he was really saying. Prudes didn't take off all their clothes and climb into a man's bed to wait for him. They didn't offer to have breast enlargement surgery to please him. Her hands were shaking so much that her cup started to rattle in its saucer. She managed to replace them on the tray and then she stood. 'I'd like to go to bed now,' she said stiffly. 'That is, if you've finished laughing at me.'

Still grinning, he retrieved her suitcase and swung it up the stairs to a warm and airy room at the top.

She perched on the edge of the bed and

watched him snap on a lamp, then stride to the door on the opposite side of the room. 'Bathroom,' he announced, pushing it open. 'Towels and things in the cabinet.'

'Thank you.'

'You're welcome.'

She'd stood up by now and, as if sensing her tension, he smiled down at her. 'You can hardly blame me for laughing,' he said, and she felt as if her insides might melt with delight from his warmth.

'I was very young,' she said huskily. 'I would never do anything like. . .like I did again.'

'Shame.' He was very close now, and his voice was very, very soft. 'Right now I'm almost disappointed.'

Poppy's eyes widened. 'Tom—'

But she didn't finish because he bent his head and kissed her. A single, stunning, brief, hard kiss on her mouth that left it burning.

Then, abruptly, it was over. 'Breakfast at seven,' he said roughly as he pulled the door shut. 'Don't be late.'

Poppy sank onto the bed again, her pulse beating so fast that it seemed to flutter. He'd kissed her. Tom had kissed her. She didn't understand, didn't understand at all.

CHAPTER EIGHT

TOM seemed tense the next morning. 'You haven't time to eat,' he snapped when Poppy wandered downstairs and peered interestedly over his shoulder at the remains of his cereal. 'If you'd got up when I banged on your door the first time you wouldn't be running so late.'

'I went back to sleep,' she admitted, running her hands through her hair to tug out the tangles, her voice muffled by the elastic band and clips in her mouth and her eyes on his mouth. But if he wasn't going to mention the kiss then she certainly wasn't. Perhaps it had been meant as a comforting gesture after her burglary. 'Sorry.'

'If a noise like that doesn't get you up then how the hell. . .?' He stopped. 'Never mind,' he said sourly. 'And don't touch that toast. Get ready. It's almost eight. Traffic's hell now.'

'I am ready.' She twisted her hair up and clipped it into place, then stuffed a piece of buttered toast into her mouth.

Impatiently he shoved his chair back and reached for his jacket and briefcase. 'Shoes?' he suggested icily. 'Planning to wear shoes today?'

Unable to talk for the food in her mouth,

185

she balanced on a chair and flexed one small stockinged foot at him soothingly.

But the gesture seemed to heighten his annoyance. 'Poppy, for God's sake! We're very late.'

Determined to stay unruffled, she ambled into the living room and retrieved her shoes from beside the couch. 'You know I'd never have guessed you were the uptight sort,' she mused. And it was true. This was a new Tom for her and it was good to see that he was not always perfectly in control—it made him infinitely more human.

'I'm not uptight,' he grated from the archway. 'I just do not like being late.'

'Neither do I,' she countered, ignoring his doubtful grunt as she bent to scoop up her bag. 'But when I am at least I don't let my blood pressure run out of control.'

'That's because everyone around you does it for you,' he snarled. He marched through the room and glared at her from the hall. 'Now get in the car.'

She clicked her tongue thoughtfully as she approached him. 'Ever considered relaxation tapes?'

He was scowling as he wrenched the front door open. 'Ever considered a lobotomy?'

Poppy spent the morning in minors but when

it quietened in the afternoon she started drifting from side to side, depending on demand. Tom's temper mellowed at work and by the time she needed to ask for his help with one of her patients he was businesslike again.

'Nineteen years old. Anterior dislocation of the shoulder,' she explained, stepping back hastily from the X-ray box, partly so that he could examine the films for himself but mostly because she always found it hard to breathe when he stood so close. 'First time. No nerve or vascular damage.'

She glanced at the patient, who lay snoring on the stretcher beside them. 'The Entonox didn't work so I gave him pethidine and Valium and—with Lucy's help—I tried to reduce it but he's too strong for me to shift. Since he's still so relaxed we thought it was worth one last attempt before a general anaesthetic.'

'Fine.'

'You're marginally stronger than me,' she added shakily. 'You might have more luck.'

'Marginally?' His eyebrows arched. 'I suppose that's one way of looking at it.' He exchanged a mocking look with Lucy, who promptly laughed. 'Considering that I could wrench your head from your body with one hand should the urge take me.'

His eyes suggested that the urge took him

quite often and, casting a baleful look towards the sister whose amusement she considered a personal betrayal, Poppy said stiffly, 'Let's just get on with it, shall we?'

Tom grinned. Taking the sleeping man's arm, he explained what he was about to do in case there remained a smidgen of consciousness. Then, while Poppy and Lucy held their patient still on the trolley, Tom applied traction to his arm then gently rotated it.

Poppy had done exactly the same thing. Her own shoulders still ached from pulling, but it was a manoeuvre that required strength. Strength that Tom obviously had, for he barely seemed to make any effort at all yet the shoulder clunked audibly back into position.

She took her patient's wrist after Tom folded the arm across to his opposite shoulder, waiting for Lucy to fit a sling and flinching at the disturbing brush of Tom's fingers as they exchanged grips. 'Sh-shall I show you the check films?'

'If you're worried.' He didn't look concerned but the pleasure she felt in his confidence of her abilities was battered when he grinned at Lucy. 'I'll leave you to keep an eye on him, Sister.' He nodded to their sedated patient. 'Make sure he isn't still comatose when we go off duty,'

Lucy smiled at her when he left. 'So things are going well with Tom?'

Well? Poppy blinked, studying her patient worriedly now. 'You're joking, aren't you?'

'He seems happy enough.'

'Hmm?' Poppy sucked in her cheeks, too distracted to reflect on that. 'Lucy, you don't think he's comatose, do you?' She dug her knuckles into the man's sternum and then, disturbed by his lack of response, did it again. 'Perhaps I overdid the pethidine. . .?'

Lucy laughed. 'Don't be silly,' she chided. 'Tom's only teasing.' Now that his arm was safely encased in a sling, she adjusted the trolley to sit their patient up. 'Michael,' she called, tapping his cheek. 'Michael, wake up now.'

To Poppy's relief, he did actually stir, although without waking up.

Lucy, though, seemed unconcerned. 'Organise the X-ray,' she told Poppy firmly. 'I'll keep an eye on him.'

Before leaving the hospital that evening—and after making sure that the young man with the shoulder injury was awake—Poppy visited Blue Ward, one of the medical wards on the second floor, sneaking surreptitiously into the acute bay.

Beneath the clear plastic of his oxygen mask

she could see that Ray Powers still looked unwell. His eyes were closed and his colour was unhealthily dusky but at least he was breathing—if barely.

Gently she touched his shoulder. 'Mr Powers?'

Slowly his heavy eyes opened, then immediately closed again, his face creasing into a weary scowl. He lifted one yellow-stained hand weakly and flicked it as if to wave her away.

Poppy hesitated. 'Do you need anything? Water? Tea? Anyone I can contact for you?'

He grunted again and this time there was no mistaking his meaning. He didn't want her there.

Telling herself that if he was well enough to be bad-tempered then he was improving, she walked slowly away from the ward towards the security building at the front of the hospital.

Mr Sweeny still had no information about her flat and it seemed that the locks weren't due to be changed or the furniture replaced until Friday at the earliest, but in the meantime there was no vacant flat for her to move into.

She had little choice but to return to Tom's— not that she was unhappy about that, she acknowledged, retrieving her Honda from outside the flat and driving it towards his home. In fact, although she hated the thought of

intruding, she decided that living in his house
was an arrangement she could get used to. Particularly if it meant any more kisses like last
night, she thought, more than a little shocked
at herself.

To her surprise the lights were on at the
house, suggesting that Tom was already home;
she'd assumed he'd be working late as usual.
When he opened the door she understood. Janet
De Beer was with him, looking extremely
startled to see Poppy.

'We're on our way out,' said Tom, shrugging
at her hesitant news about her flat not yet being
ready. 'There's ham and cheese and bread in
the kitchen if you can't manage cooking.'

He looked at the Honda, said something sca-
thing about it lowering his property value then
went to open the gates which Poppy had just
closed.

Poppy managed an awkward smile for Janet.
'I. . .my flat was burgled.'

'How inconvenient.' Wintry eyes met hers
briefly. 'Tom's always had an overdeveloped
sense of responsibility,' she added coldly.

'He's been very kind.'

'I'm sure.' Janet stepped elegantly off the
porch. 'He feels sorry for you.'

Poppy stared after her, her mouth open. He
felt sorry for her? Why?

Tom came back. He opened the car door for Janet and waited while she swung her legs graciously inside then shut the door and looked at Poppy. 'I want you up early tomorrow.'

Poppy gathered herself. 'Of course. I'm too frightened about your blood pressure to do anything else.' She watched him stride around to the other side. 'Will you be late?'

'Probably.' His hard look told her very clearly to mind her own business and involuntarily she glanced towards Janet.

'Try not to burn the house down.' Tom opened the driver's door, taking exaggerated care not to bang the side of her Honda, crookedly parked beside it. 'And, remember, breakfast at six-thirty.'

'Six-thirty.' Poppy sucked in her cheeks. That sounded very early. 'Six-thirty—sevenish,' she amended quietly as he backed past her.

But he hadn't just been trying to frighten her. A cross glare at her watch told her that it was six o'clock sharp when he pounded on her door the next morning. 'Poppy, get up.'

'Go away.'

'Up now or it's a bucket of cold water.'

'I'm up, I'm up.' She snuggled lower. 'I'm up.'

Covered with cotton and down, she didn't hear the door open—didn't hear anything until he tugged back the coverings over her head. 'Liar.'

'Ten minutes.' Irritably she ripped the duvet out of his hands and covered her face again, curling herself into a tense little ball.

But she'd underestimated his determination. 'Up,' he said tautly. 'Now!' And he promptly wrenched back all the coverings, leaving her bemused and furious.

Mutinously she lifted her head and glared at him, an uneasy night spent racked with horrible jealousy doing nothing to improve her temper. She hated him for looking so alert and refreshed, obviously straight out of the shower, his dark hair damp and his shirt so crisp that it must be freshly ironed. How dared he stay out until two twenty-five in the morning, doing heaven knows what with Janet DeBeer, yet still manage to look unbearably wonderful.

Unconsciously her fingers gripped her pillow.

'Great outfit,' he mocked, his mouth quirking as he bent and tweaked the striped fabric of her pyjamas mockingly. 'I wore similar ones at prep school.'

Violently she lashed out at him with the pillow. He was off guard so it caught him a heavy blow on the side of his face. 'Ten minutes,' she snarled, leaping to her feet and balancing on the bed. As he collapsed she continued to club the exposed side of his head mercilessly. 'Ten minutes! Was that so much to ask?'

'Yes.' He was laughing now, fending off her blows with his arms. 'Poppy, stop it. You'll destroy the pillow.'

It was true—already feathers were starting to float around, but she didn't care. All she cared about was destroying his smug, irritating self-satisfaction. Feinting a stab that made him protect his chest, she leapt to one side and brought the pillow down hard towards his undefended head.

But the move left her unbalanced, her hair loose and swinging so that it blinded her for a few seconds. When he grabbed her ankles she floundered, the pillow sliding from her grasp as she fell to the bed in a tumble of flailing limbs and breathless fury.

Immediately he was over her, laughing at her impotence as she tried to heave him away and holding her wrists so that she couldn't claw at him. 'You crazy woman,' he murmured.

Their eyes met and clung. He was warm and heavy and she stopped struggling. For a few seconds they stayed like that—still—and then she moistened parched lips and his gaze dropped to her mouth, burning her, and suddenly she couldn't breathe again.

His hands shifted, slid and tangled in her hair. Then he was lifting her closer and his head bent towards her and this was everything she'd ever dreamed about and her eyes closed with the breathless delight of it all and the last thing she heard before he kissed her was his hoarse, 'I must be mad.'

She opened her mouth eagerly, her temper forgotten—loving the urgency of him, the passionate male taste of him, the heavy weight that pressed her into the softness of the mattress.

'This isn't happening,' he muttered once after long minutes when, for a fraction of a second, he lifted his head. But she reached for his shoulders and with a groan that seemed half reluctance, half relish, he slid lower, burying his mouth in her neck—his hands fumbling with the buttons of her pyjamas.

When his mouth closed over her flesh she slid back weakly, her head twisting slowly, her mouth open and her breath coming in soft urgent pants. Everything seemed to slow. There was no urgency now—only gentle, slow exploration and the steady suckle of his mouth that was driving her mad.

She seemed to be swimming through porridge. Her limbs were heavy, her movements—

when she shifted beneath him—sluggish and dull. Her head was muzzy with the delicious male scent of him.

She was warm and cocooned and liquid and she wanted this never to stop.

Only it did.

Without warning, he lifted himself away and she was alone. 'That's enough,' he said hoarsely, dragging her jacket closed.

'Tom. . .?' Poppy's eyes blinked open dazedly and she raised herself, careless of the way her jacket was falling open again.

'No.' He levered himself completely off the bed, one hand raking his hair, and she saw determination as well as shock in the strained creases around his eyes and mouth. 'This feels wrong.'

She shivered. 'I—it felt all right to me.'

Tom swore. 'I don't mean the sex.'

Oh. Janet. Poppy slumped back into the bedding, dismally self-conscious now. She concentrated on buttoning her top because thinking of anything else was unbearable.

'I'll make breakfast.' His voice came from near the door. 'Take your time.'

And she did. For the first time he didn't comment on her lateness, merely inspected her neutrally as she sat opposite him.

She reached for the cereal. 'Janet DeBeer,' she asked tightly, filling her bowl with cereal

hoops then topping it up with milk—amazing
herself with the apparent calm ordinariness of
the gesture. 'Are you going to marry her?'

There was a brief silence during which she
kept her gaze firmly on her food. 'Janet doesn't
have anything to do with this,' he said finally.

She looked up quickly, saw wariness in his
expression but not deceit, and pressed on. This
morning she probably would have let him do
anything he'd wanted. That made her feel as if
she had some right to the truth, and she needed
that truth if she was to get on with her life. 'Are
you in love with her?'

'No.'

'Do you. . .do you feel sorry for me?'

'What?' He looked so astonished that she
was convinced. 'What on earth for?'

'It doesn't matter.' Holding herself very
stiffly, she said, 'Do you find freckles and very
small breasts repellent?'

Abruptly he lowered the spoon he'd been
about to put into his mouth. 'Don't be ridiculous.'

That wasn't an answer. She gritted her teeth.
'For your information,' she said in a brittle
voice, 'some of the greatest women in the world
are flat-chested.'

Tom frowned. 'Who?'

'Never mind "who?".' She pushed her plate

away and stood, sickeningly aware that she couldn't carry this off, not now at least. 'Try not to have a heart attack, but we were supposed to be at work half an hour ago.'

He caught up with her as she marched towards the hall, holding her coat as she shoved her arms down the sleeves. 'It was nothing to do with the way you look,' he said roughly. 'Nothing to do with other women or freckles or the size of your breasts. Just forget it. I made a mistake.'

He'd made a mistake? He'd turned her life upside down and aroused passions she'd barely conceived of but it was just a mistake? 'For goodness' sake, it's not as if I haven't been kissed before,' she managed, striving for carelessness to cover her hurt. With her eyes fixed on her shaking fingers as they fumbled at the buttons of her coat, she attempted a worldly smile. 'I thought we were both enjoying ourselves.'

There was a brief, loaded silence and then he sighed. 'Poppy, I was doing more than kissing you and you know as well as I do that it's impossible.'

'Do I?'

Firm hands on her shoulders turned her around. 'I told you when you first started that this is an important time in your career;

you need to concentrate on your work.'

He waited as if he expected her to say something, but she didn't believe his excuse and she stayed silent. Finally he frowned. 'I like my life the way it is,' he said flatly, the words driving into her hard like pieces of sharpened glass. 'I like peace and quiet and I like order and you, Poppy Brown, would drive me as mad as I would you.'

'But you wouldn't,' she protested.

'Yes, I would. We'd row constantly.'

'We'd make up.'

'Only if I didn't kill you first,' he murmured.

Bravely she lifted her chin. 'Janet DeBeer's more your type, then.'

He tapped her nose. 'I've never been tempted to throttle her, if that's what you mean. Half the time I'm with you I'm torn between strangling you and. . .' he grimaced '. . .well, punishing you in other ways,' he said softly.

Poppy met his eyes unflinchingly although inside she quivered. 'I might not mind that,' she said quietly.

'But I would.' He was very still, his eyes lighting with a speculative gleam that set alarm bells ringing in Poppy's head. 'It's strange, talking to you like this,' he mused. 'Sometimes you seem so young that I forget you're all grown up now.'

'I'm very grown up,' she whispered.

'I understand you're experienced,' he said gently, 'but, however appealing it might seem at the moment, casual sex won't do anything to improve our. . .professional relationship.'

Casual sex? Poppy felt sick. Was that what he thought she'd been offering?

'We have to work together till August,' Tom was continuing. 'Then, if you're accepted onto the rotation, you'll be attached to the National for years. It would be awkward—more than awkward, disastrous—for both of us.'

'Assuming that it ends.' Her voice was as brittle as toffee. *Casual sex*? 'Heaven knows, we might fall in love.'

'Idiot.' Maddeningly, he relaxed completely at that; eyes that had been cool and narrowed were laughing again. 'I should have known not to take you seriously.' He opened the front door and Poppy stalked outside.

'Poppy?'

She turned back, scowling. 'What?'

His dancing gaze dropped. 'Shoes?'

'Oh.' She sucked in her cheeks, lifting first one foot and then the other as the cold from the damp concrete seeped into her feet. There seemed little point in trying to maintain her dignity, but she managed to stop herself hissing at him as she pushed her way back inside.

'Try by the couch.'

'I know where they are,' she snapped, making for the stairs. But the black pumps that she'd worn the day before weren't in her room. Irritably she stomped back downstairs, ignoring his exaggerated sigh as she marched into the living room and found the shoes precisely where he'd suggested.

She avoided his gaze as she finally climbed into the car beside him. 'It must be tough,' she said though clenched teeth, 'knowing everything. Life can't hold any surprises.'

'Oh, but it does.' He was still grinning as he reversed along the drive. 'Believe me, it does.'

As soon as they arrived in Casualty Lucy asked her to see a patient in Resusc urgently. 'Just arrived,' she told her. 'Two hours of chest pain. The infarct looks like acute anterior on the ECG.'

As usual, Lucy's diagnosis was correct. The ambulance staff had already given him an aspirin, inserted a Venflon and taken blood for baseline measurements. Poppy took a quick history, examined him briefly and charted diamorphine for his pain and cyclizine for nausea for Lucy to administer. She then bleeped the medical registrar.

As dictated by hospital policy, he arrived within five minutes. He glanced at the ECG then gave her a friendly grin. 'Streptokinase ready?'

'All set,' Poppy confirmed, nodding to the pump beside the bed. The clot-dissolving drug was already connected to the patient's Venflon but the National's protocol required the approval of a medical registrar before the infusion actually started. In rare cases, but perhaps in greater numbers in future if cardiac surgery funding improved, suitable patients could proceed immediately to surgery.

Clearly not today, though, for the registrar listened to the history she'd obtained, had a few words with the patient and then started the pump.

Lucy noted the time on the casualty card. 'Fourteen minutes. Not bad.'

The sooner streptokinase could be started the better the chance was of reducing the damage to the heart muscle, but two busy doctors rushing through the initial assessment meant that there wasn't time for leisurely explanations and often patients and their relatives were left shocked and frightened.

Patients had to remain in Resusc on a monitor for the hour it took the drug to infuse, and routinely she'd started returning to them once the registrar had finished in order to explain things more fully and give them an idea about what would happen next.

'In a heart attack the blood supply to part of your heart is blocked,' she told Mr Marsh and his wife, 'and so some heart muscle is damaged. This drug dissolves the clot that makes up most of the blockage so that the blood can get through—hopefully before too much muscle dies.'

He frowned. 'I don't want to miss the daffodils. They'll be flowering soon.'

Poppy swallowed. That was obviously an oblique reference to his fear of dying. 'We can tell how much muscle has been damaged by measuring the changes in some enzymes in the blood,' she said gently. 'It takes a few days to get the full picture. You'll be in hospital for a week to ten days.'

'There's so much to do.' His wife, a small, pale woman whose face was pinched with anxiety, leaned forward on her stool. 'It's almost spring.'

'Everything is going well,' Poppy said quietly. 'You've come into hospital quickly and had the right treatment. Your blood pressure's good and your heart rhythm's normal at the moment.'

'But the garden,' his wife fretted. 'What

about the garden? Things are growing. I can't manage.'

Poppy saw from her patient's face that he still looked worried. 'A heart attack is always serious and sometimes things don't go absolutely smoothly afterwards,' she admitted, for it would be dishonest to deny that. 'But while there aren't any problems you should both just concentrate on Mr Marsh getting better. You're in the best place and you're having good treatment. I've never worked in the CCU here but I'm told the staff are superb.'

Returning to the subject of the garden, although Poppy knew that it wasn't *really* what was concerning his wife, she said, 'It's very likely that the heart specialist will test Mr Marsh on an exercise treadmill before he's discharged. He'll explain the sort of things he can do at first when he goes home. It won't take too long to build up to normal activities again.'

She must have said something right for Mrs Marsh looked marginally less distraught. Doubtfully, Poppy added, 'And if you need help around the house or garden temporarily the ward social worker may be able to give you the name of someone suitable—either to employ or get through Social Services.'

'That would be a great help.' Mrs Marsh

perked up a little further, leaving Poppy bemused.

'We would pay, mind,' Mr Marsh said firmly, looking equally relieved. 'But just to know that everything's being looked after would give me peace of mind.'

'Er...fine.' Poppy gave the couple a bright smile as she stood up. 'Well...er...relax, get better and ask if there's anything else you'd like to know.'

'Right you are, Doctor.' They both beamed at her.

She wondered back into majors, worried. Tom was at the desk and she took a deep breath before approaching him. *Casual sex?* The words still stunned her but she had to try and behave normally—and it was normal to ask for his advice.

She explained her discussion with the Marshes. 'I went through everything,' she said huskily. 'Diagnosis, treatment, what would happen at discharge—all of that—but all they could talk about was their garden. Clearly both of them are stuck in denial. I don't know what to do.'

'They might genuinely be worried about the garden.'

'That's a typical surgical attitude.' Poppy straightened. She reached across him to retrieve the next file. 'You seem to have forgotten that our reaction to illness is based on a variety of complex psychological mechanisms.'

'Says Poppy Brown, trauma surgeon in training?' He frowned doubtfully. 'Sure you wouldn't prefer psychiatry?'

'A surgeon should treat the whole patient too,' she said, flushing, not sure now whether he was serious or merely playing with her—not understanding him at all. *Casual sex?* 'Otherwise he's just a plumber.'

'Or *she*.' His gaze was enigmatic.

'Or she,' she mumbled, sure now that he was teasing her. She watched Lucy lead a woman with a blood-stained bandage around her arm into a cubicle, acknowledging the sister's signal for her to come and look. 'I'll go and suture that arm,' she told Tom. 'Keep up my *plumbing* skills.'

'Be sure to treat the whole patient.' He was grinning now, clearly enjoying her discomfort. 'And, Poppy. . .?'

His command stilled her as she was stalking away, forcing her to swivel back. 'What?'

'Tell the medical registrar about your cardiac patient,' he said quietly. 'It's the sort of thing he'd want to know.'

Oh. She was flushing again. He had listened to her seriously after all. The only thing he'd mocked was the smug way she'd been prattling on. She'd made a fool of herself. As usual. 'I'll do that,' she said stiffly, not staying around to see his response to that as she retreated hastily to the cubicle where Lucy was waiting.

Near lunchtime the medical registrar appeared in Casualty again and Poppy mentioned her worries about the Marsh couple.

'You're probably right about the denial,' the registrar said easily. 'I'll mention it to the CCU staff. They'll talk with them.' He glanced at his watch. 'I never got around to thanking you for doing that Venflon and admitting that patient for me last week when I was run off my feet. How about I treat you to lunch?'

Tom was working at a desk a few yards away and out of the corner of her eye she saw his head lift. Poppy hesitated but Tom's presence, the fact that the registrar was blond and that she could see nothing but friendliness in his expression made up her mind. 'Somewhere expensive?' she said hopefully.

He looked offended. 'Of course.' He lowered his voice. 'I thought Big Mac and maybe splash out on some fries?'

'Sounds terrific.' Her face was carefully casual as she turned slightly. 'Tom, mind if I take an early lunch?'

'No.' His expression was guarded and cool

and for a second she felt herself tense. But then he added, 'Just don't be late back. I'm in clinic most of the afternoon,' and she realised that his displeasure was only at the thought of the department being short-staffed.

'Of course,' she muttered to herself as she fetched her bag. 'Did you think he'd be jealous?'

CHAPTER NINE

LATE that afternoon Derek mentioned that his application to join the surgical rotation had been acknowledged. 'Did you get one?'

'I haven't even sent in my application,' Poppy admitted, uneasy about her tardiness. It was important to appear keen and enthusiastic—she should have applied for a position as soon as the jobs were advertised. Considering how enthusiastic she'd been a few days ago about pursuing a career in trauma, she should have updated her CV by now.

Why, then, was she hesitating? Was it because of the things Tom had said about her needing to give her future more thought? But if she failed to get onto the surgical rotation she'd leave here with no reason ever to see Tom again. The thought made her cold. 'Get over this,' she whispered harshly, reaching for a file.

'Jamie Turner, 6. Head injury,' she read. The time of arrival in Casualty was five minutes earlier.

Jamie was lying quietly on the bed, a pale, dark-haired little boy still wearing his school uniform. Wide brown eyes watched solemnly as she came towards him.

There was a thread of panic in Jamie's mother's voice when she explained what had happened. 'We went to the park to fly his kite and then he wanted a swing.' Mrs Turner soothed her son's forehead with a quivering hand as she tried to contain Jamie's squirming two-year-old sister on her lap. 'Anna was running away and I only took my eyes off him for a few seconds.'

She shifted the wriggling toddler from side to side. 'I think a bigger boy must have pushed one of the other swings into his head. Here.' She stroked the faint mark on the side of Jamie's temple, which Poppy was examining. 'He didn't even cry out. I turned around and there he was lying on the ground, and the other boy was running away. Jamie's usually such a chatter-box. I've never seen him so quiet. It frightens me.' Poppy could see tears in her eyes. 'He's going to be all right, isn't he?'

Poppy probed the small, swollen area she'd indicated, fairly confident that it didn't indicate a fracture but worried, too, by the boy's quietness. Although he was fully conscious and able to answer simple questions with prompting, he was vague and, in her experience, too well behaved for a six-year-old. 'And you're sure he wasn't knocked out?'

'Yes, at least I think so.' But she was hesitant and when Poppy darkened the room to examine Jamie's eyes she added hurriedly, 'Unless it was just for a second or two. . .'

His optic disc didn't appear swollen and his pupils responded equally when she tested him but Poppy still felt uneasy. While Lucy arranged for urgent skull X-rays in the cubicle Poppy discussed the case with the on-call radiologist, but he told her that she had to get neurosurgical approval before a CT scan of Jamie's head could be authorised. She tried paging the on-call neurosurgical registrar, and then, when there was no reply, the consultant for advice but had no luck with either.

'It's nearly six so they're probably both stuck in traffic on their way home,' the hospital telephonist said. 'They'll answer when they get to a telephone. As the patient's a child shall I bleep the paediatric registrar in the meantime?'

'Please.' Poppy inspected the X-rays while she waited for the registrar to call. She couldn't see any fracture and Jamie was unchanged. A CT scan, if the paediatric team had enough clout to insist on it and if it was normal, would make her feel happier about sending him to the observation ward and she hunched over the phone, tapping her fingers on the bench as she waited.

Lucy was clutching Jamie's sister Anna, skilfully containing the child's tiny hands to avoid her hair being pulled. 'No luck?'

Poppy grimaced. 'The paed's reg must be busy in Maternity,' she said tensely. 'She's usually much quicker than this.' Looking at Lucy, she sensed, rather than heard, Tom return to the department and when she turned around he was walking towards them.

'Problems?'

Briefly she filled him in.

'And you're worried about the child?'

'Yes.' Poppy walked with him to the cubicle. 'I'm not convinced he wasn't knocked out although, apart being quiet, there's nothing else to put my finger on.'

She introduced him and stood to one side as he talked to Mrs Turner, impressed by the easy confidence of his manner and the calm way in which he both elicited the information he needed and calmed her at the same time so that the high threadiness in her voice settled. Then he squatted beside Jamie and questioned him about school and football, all the while examining him—briefly, yet with a fluent thoroughness that Poppy envied.

When he stood his face was very serious. 'We're going to scan Jamie's head,' he said firmly, and Mrs Turner nodded so matter-of-factly that Poppy wondered if it was only she who could hear his urgency. 'It won't hurt but I want you to come with us.'

Instead of waiting for a porter, he lifted the subdued Jamie into his arms. 'Lucy, ring CT and tell them we're on our way. Poppy, fetch a resusc trolley and come with me.'

A resuscitation trolley? Poppy's mouth dried. Did he think Jamie was that ill?

Quickly she collected the equipment and notes and met them by the lifts. Tom cleared the first one to arrive, asking the passengers to wait for the next one. While they ascended towards X-ray he told Jamie what the scan would involve. 'It's like being in a rocket-ship,' he explained, 'only you don't go anywhere. You lie very still and it turns around you.'

The child managed only a wan nod and Poppy looked at Tom but he was watching Jamie.

The lift took them to the the X-ray department on the fourth floor, and the radiologist she'd spoken with earlier was waiting for them. A radiographer took Jamie from Tom and quickly lifted him into position, helped by a nurse, while another nurse escorted his mother outside where she'd sit and wait with her.

From behind the control panel where Poppy

stood, Jamie looked tiny—two thin legs poking out of the large white ring that surrounded his upper body. The atmosphere in the room was tense and now that Mrs Turner could no longer see him Tom looked very concerned.

'Thick cuts to start,' he said grimly. 'If there is a problem, it'll be right temporal.'

The radiologist nodded. 'Contrast?'

'Only if we don't see anything.'

The machine took cross-sectioned pictures of Jamie's head and the first few sections showed the top of his brain which, to Poppy's eyes, looked slightly bloated and asymmetrical. When the next scans appeared she paled. They showed a collection of blood exactly where Tom had predicted. The blow Jamie had had to his head had obviously damaged the blood vessels beneath the skull and they'd begun to bleed and that bleeding was putting pressure on the fragile tissue of the boy's brain.

His eyes still on the emerging pictures, Tom picked up the telephone and asked the operator to page the on-call neurosurgeon urgently. He then rang the emergency anaesthetist and theatre staff and told them to expect Jamie.

'I need help.' The nurse who'd been with Jamie hauled the trolley out of the machine. 'He's fitting.'

Tom and Poppy raced to the bed. Obeying

Tom's instructions, she managed to get a line into one frail arm while Tom held Jamie's jaw and fitted an oxygen mask over his mouth and nose.

The fit was confined to Jamie's left side and was of short duration but when he didn't regain consciousness Tom swiftly inserted an endo-tracheal tube and began to bag him, driving oxygen into his lungs—reminding Poppy that that was one way of reducing brain swelling in an emergency.

'Neurosurgeon's on his way in.' While they'd been busy the radiologist had answered the call. 'Fifteen minutes tops.'

Tom nodded acknowledgement as he raised Jamie's eyelids and inspected his pupils. 'Let's go,' he said tightly, lifting the oxygen cylinder he was using onto the trolley and steering it towards the door. 'We can't wait.'

An anaesthetist met them outside theatres and took over the bagging of Jamie as they swung through the doors and directly into the anaes-thetic room, where more of the team was waiting.

Tom took the scans from Poppy and slammed them up onto the X-ray board. While the anaes-thetists worked around him he bent over Jamie's head, marker pen in hand, indicating where he'd make his incisions. 'Poppy, you'll have to speak to his parents,' he said tightly. 'Get the consent signed.' Candid blue eyes met hers briefly. 'Prepare them for every outcome.'

By the time she got back to X-Ray Jamie's father had arrived and the couple sat with Anna, their hands gripped fiercely together, while Poppy explained as gently as she could that the only way they might save their son's life was to operate immediately.

She took them up to the small relatives' room attached to main Theatres and stayed with them while they waited. Mr Turner mechanically sipped the cups of sweet tea she offered him but his wife left hers untouched, cuddling her sleeping toddler and seeming to need to talk. Poppy heard about Jamie's delivery, his first smile, learning to walk and starting school, how good he was with Anna and how well he was going with his reading.

When Tom opened the door they all leapt up. Still in his theatre blues, he looked achingly handsome but she saw the weariness and strain around his eyes. To her relief, though, there was quiet calm in the gaze that met hers, before turning to the Turners. 'Jamie's in the intensive care unit,' he said simply. 'I'll take you to him.'

On the way he told them that they'd succeeded in draining the clot from his brain but that it might be days or even weeks before they could predict how well he'd recover. He warned them about how Jamie would look, a warning that was warranted because even Poppy was shocked by the sight of the thin, tiny figure on the bed, dwarfed by the equipment that surrounded him.

His head was encased in bandages from which blood-lined drains protruded and a tube through his nose connected him to a ventilator that pulsed regularly as it fed oxygen into his lungs. Another tube drained his bladder, several lines led from his arms to bags of fluid suspended above him and a monitor attached to one of the lines and to his chest bleeped his heartbeat and displayed his blood pressure.

Tom pulled chairs across for Jamie's parents so that they could hold their son's hands. 'Everything you see here is normal,' he told them quietly when their bewildered gazes strayed across the machines. 'All designed to make it easier to care for Jamie.'

The neurosurgical consultant who was looking after Jamie now approached them, and after introducing him to Jamie's parents Tom took Poppy's elbow and steered her out of the unit. 'Give me ten minutes to change,' he told her. 'Meet you in Casualty.'

Instead of going straight to the department to wait for him, Poppy visited Blue Ward.

'I'm very sorry,' the sister said kindly when she asked if Ray Powers had been moved. 'He died this morning. We didn't know who to notify. Are you a relative?'

'No.' Poppy explained who she was and the sister gave her a few more details.

Afterwards she walked stiffly back down the stairs. What an awful day this had been. First poor little Jamie and now this. 'You knew he was going to die,' she told herself sensibly. But it didn't help. She'd barely known the man—he hadn't liked her, he'd been grumpy and uncooperative and she doubted whether he'd appreciate her sentiments—yet still she felt dismay at his death.

Not grief exactly, not the sort of grief she felt when young people were injured or died—children like Jamie or, as she'd seen during her medical attachment, young adults suffering, their youthful bodies ravaged by leukaemias or AIDS.

The overwhelming emotion she recognised was regret. Regret that she and medicine had failed this man.

Tom was waiting in Casualty when she arrived and they walked out to the car park together. 'I didn't realise things could go wrong so quickly,' she said, shivering at the memory of how Jamie had deteriorated in CT. 'And I couldn't get hold of anyone. If you hadn't been there. . .'

'A general surgeon would have operated,' he said flatly. 'There's nothing magical about it. The important thing is to suspect the injury and *you* did that.'

But he was the one who'd made things happen. 'Is brain damage. . .likely?'

'It's possible.' His mouth was tight as he held the car door open for her. 'There was a lot of oedema and the tone on his left side's still abnormal, but his plantar's down.'

An upgoing plantar reflex was a sign of brain damage so as long as it stayed down there was a greater likelihood that he'd make a good recovery, and Poppy seized on that hope.

They drove home in silence, Tom as subdued as she. Neither of them had much appetite so they shared a cheese omelette and afterwards he retreated to his study to do some work while she sat alone, staring into the fire and thinking.

When Tom came back she was crying. She hadn't meant to cry—rarely ever cried—and, embarrassed that he'd caught her, she dabbed frantically at her cheeks with a soggy tissue.

'Oh, Poppy.' It was like a long sigh. He sat beside her and drew her forward so that her head rested against his chest, one of his hands rubbing slowly across her back. 'His chances aren't so bad,' he soothed. 'We operated early and you know how often children astonish us with their resilience. I've seen worse cases than Jamie recover normally.'

'It's not just that.' Even in the state she was in she knew that it was dangerous to stay to close to him and she levered herself away, needing to talk now—needing to keep her head clear. She *was* upset about Jamie and for his family and Tom's words gave her some comfort, but Ray Powers bothered her too—made her question the medicine she practised—and she told Tom about his death.

'It's so frustrating. Sometimes it seems as if all we're doing is scratching together to patch up disasters. We're not doing anything to stop things going wrong in the first place.'

'It's not that easy.'

'But it should be.' He seemed very close and she slid back on the couch, his nearness making her ache for something she knew she shouldn't. 'We should be educating people more, teaching them how to keep themselves healthy!'

'In an ideal world.' He sounded impatient. 'You have to be practical. As a surgeon you're too busy coping with "disasters" to deal with anything else.'

'There has to be time,' she insisted because she refused to think of herself as someone who simply waited for things to go wrong. 'There has to be.'

Tom sighed. 'Poppy, you're going into the wrong job,' he said. 'The fact is that in surgery there isn't time for anything but the job in hand, and there never will be.'

Tears were prickling at her eyes again and furiously she tried to blink them away, uncomfortably aware that there was self-pity, too, in her misery—something she was ashamed of. Tom clearly didn't think she was cut out for surgery and his opinion meant a great deal to her. 'I'm sorry.' She sniffed, lowering her head when she realised that he'd seen her tears. 'I'm not usually such an emotional wreck.'

'It hasn't been a good day.' He ruffled her hair. 'And you're right to question the way we work—we all do. It's part of the process of becoming a better doctor.'

'I guess.'

One firm hand tilted her chin, forcing her to look at him. 'You are a good doctor, Poppy. Despite everything else, you are that.'

She swallowed heavily. 'Despite everything else. . .?'

His mouth quirked. 'Despite your disorganisation,' he teased. 'Despite your idealism and your silly books and your funny, fairy-tale way of looking at the world.'

I love you. The words sounded so loudly in her head that she recoiled and, horrified that she might have spoken aloud, she leapt from the couch, spinning away until she was standing beside the fire and staring at him. 'No.'

'No, what?' Tom was frowning at her. 'No, you don't look at the world that way?'

'No,' said Poppy in a brittle voice, her thundering pulse settling as slowly she began to understand that she hadn't actually said the words. 'Just no. . .' She could barely look at him, her gaze flickering towards the couch, the rug, the floor. I love him. I love him. 'I'm going to bed.'

'Poppy, wait!' They reached the door at the same time but his arm across the frame stopped her flight. 'After this morning I don't want you to think. . .' He stopped. 'I wasn't going to touch you again.'

'I know that.' God! She froze. 'That wasn't why I. . .'

'You were frightened.'

Her head snapped up. 'No,' she managed hoarsely. 'No, not frightened.' But he was right. It was her reaction that frightened her, not him. 'I was. . .' She swallowed heavily, breathless now for he was very, very, close and she could hardly think and she loved him and his eyes were more brilliant and more glittering blue than she'd seen before and she loved him, she loved him. 'I was. . .' She pulled herself straight. 'I'd never be frightened of you.'

'That's always been your mistake.' Not giving her time to understand, he backed her against the wall. One strong hand cupped her throat and chin and lifted her face and then, abruptly, he kissed her. Not a probing, passionate kiss like before, but a short, hard, almost angry kiss—then another and another and then her throat and her neck and then her mouth again, but this time slower, gentler, and she was in heaven.

His mouth tracked to her ear and she shivered. 'You were a witch today,' he said hoarsely. 'When you flirted with that registrar I wanted to kiss you senseless.'

Poppy swallowed, delighted—seduced by the thought that she had the power to affect him like that. 'You were jealous?'

'As you wanted me to be.' He took her mouth again in a long, demanding kiss and his hands were everywhere—in her hair, at her breasts, sliding under the soft wool of her jumper. When he lifted his head she was dizzy. 'I'm beginning to think that the only way to stop this is to get it out of our systems.'

His words jolted her and she twisted her head away. She loved him. 'I can't,' she whispered.

'I can't. Not just once or twice. Not casually
as if it doesn't mat—'

'How long?' His fingers were lifting her
jumper now and they were warm and gentle
and she couldn't bear to push them away. 'A
week? A month?'

A month from now seemed endless—more
than enough time to convince him that they
were meant to be together—but this was too
important, and still she held back. 'Not enough.'

Impatient hands tugged the jumper over her
head, baring her breasts. 'You might be right,'
he murmured, the words muffled by the pale
curve of her flesh as he sought one tiny taut
peak. 'Let me take you to bed.'

Bed. It sounded wonderful. Every molecule
of her being wanted to believe that this might
be for ever and so she let herself believe. She
opened her mouth to his kiss again, loving him,
letting him lift her, balance her in his arms,
loosen her skirt.

But the brush of fabric across her thighs still
startled her and Poppy clutched for the skirt,
but he just laughed at her. He tugged it away,
his mouth lowering to stop her protest as he
teased her, roused her, eased her wavering
doubts, carried her towards the stairs and then
to his bedroom.

He switched on a lamp and, befuddled by his

kisses, she lay dazed when he lowered her to his bed. This was going to happen. She loved him and this was really going to happen. Her breath coming in quick shallow pants, Poppy watched mutely as he dealt swiftly with his own clothes until her eyes widened on the very masculine strength of his desire as he followed her onto the bed.

She sat up, alarmed. 'Tom——'

'Shush.' Smoothing back her hair, he cupped her face and then he was kissing her again, enchanting kisses that left her hot and restless and her breathing ragged.

But still something niggled. Twisting her head away, she said hoarsely, 'There's something I——'

'Don't you like this?' He slid lower, tasting her, lingering on her breasts, bathing them with moist tugging warmth. 'Hmm?'

'Um. . .yes. Oh, yes.' Poppy shifted beneath him, breathlessly restless as sharp, aching shards of sensation peeled from his suckling and pierced her, teased deep into the folds of her flesh.

He left her breasts and she felt his mouth at her stomach—licking, teasing—then at her thighs, and then. . . Poppy's eyes widened abruptly and she clawed at his shoulders, wriggling. 'No. . .'

At first he resisted but when she started to panic he returned to her, forcing her flat again and laughing at her anxiety. 'Relax,' he said, his voice low and rasping against her throat and making her shiver.

But when he seemed about to swivel back to her thighs she cried out, alarmed again, and once more he laughed. 'So you are a little prude after all.' His grin was wicked as his fingers probed the moistness his mouth had sought, making her head spin even as her body arched towards him.

'Tom, wait. . .' Any more and she wouldn't be able to think at all, let alone make any sense, and unless he knew there'd be pain—unbearable pain—and she needed more talk, more reassurance about his feelings.

Pushing his hand away, she twisted onto her side and hold him at bay with her bent knees, two small palms against his chest. 'You have to understand,' she hissed urgently. 'I've never ridden a horse.'

But his face registered blank incomprehension and, instead of being overcome with tenderness, he laughed. 'Neither have I, you fruit cake.' Unperturbed, he reached for her, easily overcoming her puny strength to tumble her over on top of him. 'Shut up and come here.'

But she struggled free of the hand that urged her down to him, clamping her knees around his legs to stop him pulling her forward. 'You know what horse-riding is supposed to do to a woman, don't you? Horse-riding, gymnastics, all those things.'

He expelled his breath heavily. 'Tell me about it later,' he muttered, reaching up again to suckle one tight little breast. 'Let me taste you.'

For a brief moment her eyes closed weakly and she was tempted to let events take their natural course, but somehow she found the strength to force them open. Frantically she wriggled up again, pushing his taunting mouth away. 'My hymen,' she said loudly, holding his head between her hands and keeping everything very clinical now so that there would be absolutely no misunderstanding, 'is intact.'

His face, his hands, his body—everything—went very still. 'What?'

Poppy flushed at his incredulous expression but she kept her head lifted. 'I even have difficulty with. . .when I have my period,' she mumbled, her courage faltering at his darkening expression. 'I—I thought you should know. In advance. Um. . .so you'll be careful.'

'I'll be a damn sight more than careful.' His face was grim now and he tipped her off him, ignoring her indignant squeal as he hauled the sheet out from beneath her to cover her, tucking it tightly around her despite her best efforts to resist him. 'What the hell did you think you were playing at?'

'I thought *we* were playing.' Trapped and protected like a mummy in the cocoon of the sheet, she was suddenly brave. She let her eyes drop pointedly to his abruptly fading arousal. 'I thought men liked the idea of being first. I didn't realise it made them impotent.'

The hands tightened fractionally. 'I am not impotent,' he grated.

She lifted sceptical eyebrows. 'That's what it looks li—'

One hand released her body and clamped across her mouth. 'I wouldn't,' he warned tightly.

Poppy swallowed heavily and after a few tense seconds he took his hand away, swinging around so that he sat beside her. 'Now,' he grated, 'let's start at the beginning. What about the blonds? So many you couldn't remember?'

She flushed. 'I. . .exaggerated. A little.'

Tom swore. 'And your flirtation with that psychiatrist? Your offer to go and stay with one of your lovers? Your assurances that you were so grown up?' He looked furious now. 'For

God's sake, you practically propositioned me this morning!'

'I. . .' She didn't know what to say. Explaining that she hadn't wanted him to know that she was attracted to him would be as damaging as telling him that she loved him so much that she couldn't fight her need for him. 'I don't think I actually propositioned you,' she said hesitantly.

'Give me a break.' His hands clenched and he glared at her throat as if he were contemplating strangling her. 'Even you are not that innocent.' Then he leaned forward, his elbows braced on his knees and his face lowered to his palms. 'I knew I shouldn't be touching you,' he said grimly. 'I knew that from the start but you were just so damned—' His face tightened. 'For God's sake, Poppy, I thought—I *assumed*—you at least knew what you were doing!'

'I did!'

But the eyes that lifted to hers were frosted like blue chips of ice. 'What if I hadn't been able to stop?'

Poppy blinked. 'I didn't ask you to stop—only to be careful. I'm not good with pain—I take paracetamol to have my hair cut!'

But he scowled, her miserable attempt at humour falling deathly flat. 'For a woman,' he grated, 'the first time should be special. You don't just choose someone at random.' Every controlled movement furious again, he surged off the bed and strode towards the window on the far side of the room. He spun to glare at her, his face set and his arms folded. 'I can't believe you could be so irresponsible.'

'I am not irresponsible,' she raged. Why was she the only one to blame here? This hadn't been her idea. 'And I did not just "choose someone at random".'

Flushing hotly, she pushed herself up—clutching the sheet that was her only covering as she leapt from the bed and marched to confront him. She snatched at the bottom of the cotton as it gathered round her ankles, almost tripping her. 'For your information, Tom Grainger, I happen to...be very f-fond of you,' she said agitatedly, staring boldly into his darkly shuttered expression. 'Goodness knows why!'

The sheet tangled her legs again and she aimed a vicious, frustrated kick at the wall, forgetting that her foot was bare and crying aloud when it connected with the brick. 'And you don't deserve it,' she sobbed, clutching her injured toes as she hopped in pain. 'You're a cynical, know-it-all bast—' But even in her fury she couldn't say the word and instead it just lingered there between them, half-spoken, but both of them understanding.

Tom's mouth tightened. He reached for her swelling foot, forcing her to hop backwards and sit on the bed. 'At least they're not broken,' he grated. 'Stay there. I'll get ice.'

A few minutes later he was back, a broad towel tied securely round his waist. 'I might even l-love you,' she said miserably, peering up at him as he held her leg in the air and twined an ice-filled cloth around her toes. 'One day. If you were very nice to me.'

'That,' he said tightly, his mouth set in a hard line, 'will never happen. Your problem is that your head's stuck in the clouds.'

She paled. 'You don't believe me.'

Roughly he hauled the pillow from beneath her head, adding it to the other and propping her throbbing foot on both while he held the ice on it. 'You're not believable.'

'What if I told you my heart aches for you?' she said bravely.

His eyes lifted briefly to the ceiling. 'I'd say it wasn't your *heart* that's aching,' he said flatly. 'You're a twenty-five-year-old virgin. No wonder you're a little. . .frustrated.'

The toes of her other foot curled furiously. 'There's no need for crudity,' she stormed.

'Says the woman who climbs into my bed in the middle of the night,' he taunted. 'You may be intact but you're no Snow White, Poppy Brown.'

'And you're no Prince Charming,' she spat, glibly mixing her fairy-tales—wincing in protest as he shifted the ice cubes. 'And, for your information, that was a very long time ago. I'm a different person now.'

'You haven't exactly gone out of your way to defend your honour,' he said nastily. 'Consider yourself lucky—'

'Lucky?' She threw her arms into the air. 'Huh! If this is how it feels to be lucky I'm not rushing to buy any lottery tickets.'

'You were the one who kicked the wall.'

'I'm not talking about my foot!'

His mouth twitched. 'Now who's being crude?' he said softly. 'Hmm?'

'Shut up.' But his grin was infectious and after a few seconds she gave up trying to resist and collapsed back on the bed, her mouth melting into a rueful smile. 'You're horrible,' she said weakly as she closed her eyes, exhausted by the evening's traumas. 'Life's so unfair. It hurts. I need morphine.'

'You need ice and elevation,' he said bluntly, rapping her shin briskly with his knuckles when she twisted her foot to peer at the swollen discoloration more worriedly. 'And, for God's sake, keep it still!' He left her. 'I'll get some dressings. Stay there.'

But as soon as she heard him on the stairs Poppy hobbled to the bathroom. It was much larger than her own and, despite her misery, she admired its huge, inviting bath, separate shower cubicle and beautiful marble cabinets.

After washing her hands, she frowned at the dismal reflection in the mirror. She looked like a rag doll—all long straggly hair, pale face and big worried eyes. 'With this looking at him, no wonder he lost his enthusiasm,' she said bleakly.

But splashing her face with cold water and pinching her cheeks to give herself a little colour didn't make much difference. She found a plastic box of dental floss in a cabinet drawer, pulled out a length and fastened the hair that had tumbled around her shoulders into a ragged ponytail. 'Poppy Brown, glamour queen,' she muttered bitterly. 'Not.'

'What the hell are you doing?'

Poppy jumped, promptly put her weight onto her injured foot and then caught her breath with pain.

Tom swore. Unceremoniously he jerked her into his arms and carried her into the bedroom, dumping her onto the bed and watching expressionlessly as she clutched at the sheet again to cover herself. 'I told you to stay where you were.'

'I needed the bathroom.' She was flushing.

'You should have waited.' He sat on the bed with her and lifted her foot onto his thigh.

She propped herself on her elbows and watched his briskness as he examined her, saw his concentration as he buddy-strapped her aching toes, and it seemed like a dream that she'd lain here, just a short while ago, in his arms.

He didn't love her, she realised, her heart a cold little lump in her chest. If he did he would have made her his by now. But until she stopped seeing him every day at work there was no point trying to fight or deny or get over her own feelings. That would have to come later, much later.

However ludicrous it might be, the thought that she could delay the agony was vaguely cheering and she brightened a little.

He wound two layers of soft dressing around her foot and tucked away the loose ends. Then his fingers stilled against the tingling skin of her ankle and he looked at her.

Looked at her for perhaps ten—perhaps twenty—seconds, but to Poppy it seemed endless. Her breath became shallow and rapid, her pulse thundered and her legs quaked and trembled so much that she knew he must feel them. She loved him so much that it was as if her heart had heated up to boiling again and at any moment might break through her chest.

'If it would help,' she said huskily, 'I could try horse-riding.'

Tom clicked his tongue. 'Fool,' he said softly. 'It's not the technicality——it's the principle.' He released her foot and then was up, brisk again now as he bent and lifted her. 'Bed for you,' he said firmly. 'Alone.'

CHAPTER TEN

THE next morning Tom banged on Poppy's door at six, again at six-thirty, then got cross with her when she dawdled over breakfast and still looked annoyed when he bundled her into his car at seven-thirty. 'You're not driving,' he insisted. 'The Honda stays here until you've had that foot X-rayed.'

'I keep telling you it's perfectly all right,' she stormed, for they'd been arguing that point and several others for the last half-hour. 'It's bruised, nothing more. You're a surgeon, for goodness' sake. Can't you see it's a soft tissue injury, not a fracture?'

'Admittedly it doesn't look that bad this morning,' he said grimly, reversing past the house, 'but it's obviously still painful.'

'Not as painful as explaining to everyone in Casualty how and why I did it,' she said tersely. 'Unless you'd like me to do just that?'

His scowl when he returned from locking the gates told her that he'd understood her threat. 'You are a menace,' he said tightly. 'You should be locked up.'

'And you just can't bear not getting your own

way,' she snapped, refusing to let him bully her.

'You'd rather be in pain than do what I suggest.'

She gritted her teeth. 'It's not that bad.'

'You can barely walk.'

'You always exaggerate.'

'*I* exaggerate?' Exasperated blue eyes glared at her when the car stopped at the next set of lights. 'Says the women who claimed a hundred lovers.'

'I never mentioned a number.' Poppy scowled at him. 'Besides, I only lied because you were so smugly sure I fancied you.'

'Smug!' he raged. 'Hardly! Those big green eyes had been fluttering at me all afternoon.'

'I had conjunctivitis,' she countered smoothly.

'Pity you haven't got *laryngitis* now.'

They bickered all the way to the National and then all the way from the car park to Casualty. They were still arguing when they reached the SHOs' common-room. 'You're having that X-ray if I have to throw you over my shoulder,' Tom warned.

'I haven't broken anything.' Poppy stomped her foot at him to prove it. It wasn't painless, admittedly, for the toes were badly bruised, but she wasn't in agony. 'Are you blind?'

'You're limping and you winced.'

'You're not my doctor,' she snarled. 'I haven't consulted you.'

Lucy's office door opened. 'For heaven's sake, you two, you're worse than my children.' But despite the words she looked pleased. 'Why not kiss and make up?'

'Oh, for God's sake!' Tom scowled at Poppy. 'Can't you keep your mouth shut about anything?' He jerked open the door to his own office, then slammed it behind him.

Poppy winced. 'Lucy, you've got this all wrong,' she whispered. 'He doesn't want anything to do with me. He thinks I'd ruin his life.'

But Lucy merely smiled an irritatingly knowing smile and disappeared back into her office.

Tom banished her to minors that day. Poppy was busy and saw very little of him. Late in the afternoon Mr Sweeny called to say that her flat would be ready by ten the next morning, Saturday. 'All set for the. . .er. . .weekend,' he told her.

'Thank you.' Poppy was frowning when she lowered the receiver, not sure how she felt about leaving Tom's. Certainly it wouldn't be easy to stay—not after last night and with the way they'd argued this morning—but still she'd miss him desperately. Today was the last day they'd be working together for the next eight weeks. From Monday she started night duty and, apart from the brief hand-over time when their shifts overlapped, she wouldn't see him at all.

When the shift changed at six she stayed half an hour extra to help with the backlog of work, then went to find Tom.

'If it's urgent you could try ICU,' Lucy told her, her eyes twinkling mischievously when she spotted Poppy looking for him. 'I know they wanted his advice about a case.'

Poppy had intended calling into the paediatric side of the unit anyway to see Jamie so, rather than waiting for Tom in Casualty, she limped upstairs. At lunchtime the ICU registrar had told her that they were reducing Jamie's sedation and she was keen to see if he was waking.

Tom was busy with several other doctors around one of the adult beds. He looked up at her entry and their eyes met, but she turned away and slid through the plastic doors into the children's section.

'Nothing's happened yet.' Jamie's parents sat beside the bed, clutching the child's small hand, and Poppy saw sick fear in his mother's anxious gaze. 'They said if he didn't wake immediately it might take days. . .or longer.'

'But his blood count was normal.' Jamie's father was unshaven, his hair dishevelled from where he must have been running his hands through it, but he seemed to be clutching for hope where his wife hesitated. 'That's good, isn't it?'

Poppy didn't have the heart to tell him that it was probably irrelevant. 'He looks a little better,' she said softly, telling herself that it was true. 'Besides, I'm sure he needs rest to recover properly.'

Tom came up behind her, making the hairs on the back of her neck prickle. 'Dr Brown's right,' he said quietly. He squeezed Jamie's foot and although the child didn't withdraw from the touch Poppy saw his toes dip as Tom's thumb brushed his sole. 'He won't wake until he's ready and we can't hurry nature.'

'Nature.' Jamie's mother's eyes closed as she considered that, and when she opened them again there was some brightness where earlier they'd been dull. 'That's a nice way of thinking about it,' she said softly. 'We're waiting for nature.'

As Poppy and Tom washed their hands Poppy said, 'His toe went down when you tested it. Wouldn't it be up by now if there's serious brain damage?'

'He wouldn't breathe when they tried to wean him,' Tom answered quietly, 'so things are not so straightforward.'

'Oh.' She swallowed. Hence the reason he

was still being ventilated. That was bad news, very bad news. 'When will they try again?'

'Tomorrow morning.' Tom passed her a paper towel. 'Did Sweeny speak to you?'

'My flat will be ready tomorrow,' she confirmed.

'Tomorrow?' Tom's brows drew together. He was walking while Poppy limped beside him along the corridor and suddenly he stopped. 'I thought it was going to be tonight?'

'He said something about the new door not being fitted till nine tomorrow.'

Tom didn't look very pleased and Poppy felt awful. Obviously he'd hoped to get rid of her tonight. 'I——I could stay somewhere else.'

'Don't be ridiculous.' His gaze dropped to her foot. The swelling was still obvious above the curve of her shoe and there was satisfaction in his face when he looked up at her face. 'It's not getting any better.'

'Or worse,' Poppy muttered, forcing herself to walk normally.

For dinner Tom grilled salmon and served it with salad. The food was delicious but Poppy was tense and had little appetite and Tom barely spoke.

Afterwards, when she stood to clear the plates, he scowled at her black dress. 'Are you wearing anything under that thing?'

Poppy lifted a defensive hand to cover the breast where his gaze lingered. 'Of course I am,' she said fiercely, for she would never, never admit to him that she didn't even own a bra. 'Pervert!'

'Exhibitionist.' His grimness told her that he knew she was lying. 'For a virgin, you're not exactly overburdened with modesty.'

'If I had as much modesty as you have chivalry,' she said acidly, 'I'd be naked on the table.'

'Might as well be.' His fierce blue gaze dropped to her buttocks as she bent to scrape the plates. 'It's practically transparent.'

She straightened abruptly and glanced down, reassured by the thickness of the dark cotton. 'Don't talk nonsense.'

'I won't talk at all.' He pushed his chair back. 'I'm going out.

She tried not to follow him—tried to stay still—but the effort was too much, and seconds later she ran after him and caught him as he shrugged into his coat. 'Where. . .? Are you going out with Janet?'

He stilled and she knew she was right. Something inside her shrivelled. 'H-have a nice time,' she said huskily.

An hour later a phone that refused to stop ringing dragged her from the bath where she'd

fled, seeking warmth. 'Poppy, it's me, Tom.'
There was a long pause and then he said,
'Janet's a colleague, that's all. We've been
meeting because we're working on a paper
together.' There was another pause then he said,
'I'm at work. I've a backlog of paperwork, as
well as some research to finish. I'll probably
stay all night.'

'Thanks.' Poppy's legs felt weak and she
sank slowly to the floor, her back braced against
the wall.

'This doesn't change anything,' he growled.

'I know.' She closed her eyes and leaned her
head back. 'I know.'

She heard him come home very early the next
morning. She got up, wrote a polite note,
thanking him for his hospitality, and crept out.

Security had done a good job on her flat. The
front door had been completely replaced, and
instead of one flimsy lock she now had to use
two very solid-looking keys to open it. Inside,
they'd not only tidied and cleaned but also
replaced much of the furniture with new, albeit
unfashionable items, equipped all the windows
with locks and fitted bars to the bathroom
louvres.

It was Saturday but Mr Sweeny answered
when she rang Security to thank him. 'Pleased

it. . .er. . .meets with your approval, Doctor. Mr Grainger insisted about the windows and the new door and the extra locks, of course. I did. . . er. . .tell him about our budgetary difficulties, mind, particularly since he wanted it done in such a hurry, but he. . .er. . .well, I'm sure you know all the rest.'

Poppy was quite sure she didn't. 'He. . .er. . . insisted. . .?'

'Well, as long as he's. . .er. . .paying, I've no objections to doing the work,' he said chirpily. 'Keeps us out of mischief, miss. . .er. . . Doctor.'

So Tom had paid for this?

'Oh, yes,' Mr Sweeny said when she asked directly. 'Personal cheques. One moment there, Doctor.' She heard a rustling. 'Number nine, four, six. . .er. . .'

'Never mind,' Poppy said hastily, mortified. Tom had been so keen to get rid of he that he'd paid for the work himself! 'Thank you, Mr Sweeny,' she added faintly. 'Still nothing on the suit, I suppose?'

'Not as yet.' He clicked his tongue. 'But we've kept your. . .er. . .drawing. Looks. . . er. . .rather nice on our wall.'

Casualty on Monday night was very different to the Casualty she was used to from day duty.

While there was enough to keep both herself and Derek busy the pace of work was more leisurely, with never more than half a dozen patients waiting to be seen. At eight next morning Tom arrived, along with Kim and Paul who were now covering the days.

Tom being there made her nervous, and as she handed over the patients listed on the whiteboard in majors her hands were shaking so much that she kept them tucked behind her back.

Afterwards he dismissed her hesitant attempt to thank him for paying for the work on her flat. 'It wasn't expensive,' he muttered, flicking though some waiting files and only giving her half his attention. 'Forget it. How's your foot?'

'B-better.'

'Tom, possible aneurysm arriving one minute. Hi, Poppy.' Lucy gave her a distracted smile. 'Fifty-year-old known ischaemic heart disease via the ambulance.'

'Coming.' Tom frowned at Poppy. 'Go home and sleep,' he said briskly. 'You look exhausted.'

For the rest of the week and into the next she saw him occasionally when she visited Jamie Turner in ICU but otherwise only for a few minutes each morning when she handed over her night's work.

'I'm giving up on our sexy consultant,' Kim told her one morning after hand-over when Tom was busy in Resusc. 'I've been following him around like a love-sick sheep for weeks now and he still hasn't noticed.'

Poppy doubted that. Tom was nothing if not perceptive. 'Perhaps that's wise,' she whispered, wincing at the irony of the advice.

'I'm not used to men not falling down in front of me—it's never happened before.' The blonde girl grinned. 'But Tom is *definitely* not interested. Nice as anything, totally impersonal.' She sighed dramatically, then perked up. 'Derek's cute, isn't he?'

Was he? Poppy looked blank.

The other girl laughed. 'Poppy Brown, take care you don't become an old maid,' she teased. 'There's more to life than work, you know.'

'There's more to life than work,' Poppy told Derek that night when, as usual, he retreated to his textbooks as soon as there was a lull. 'Kim's a nice girl, don't you think?'

Before she could probe any further one of the staff nurses came to fetch her. 'Fifty-four-year-old man with epilepsy,' she was told. 'Fell against a concrete step during a fit tonight.

Swollen face and black eye. Looks like he's broken his cheek-bone.'

When Poppy X-rayed his face she found that he'd fractured his malar bone. The man had recently arrived from Bangladesh and spoke very little English so they communicated through his son. She explained that he would need surgery in a few days to elevate the fracture. 'How about this eye?' She waited for the son to translate. The area around his right eye was so swollen and bruised that it had closed over. 'Any pain, Mr Ullah?'

'A little,' came the reply finally. 'Not much.'

But Poppy worried. Sometimes with this kind of fracture the eye could be damaged. 'Can he read this eye-chart?' She held her hand over his good eye and explained that he should try with the other one.

Although her patient was very obliging it took time before he understood what was required and longer to prise his sore eye gently open.

But there was no question that his vision in the swollen eye was reduced, compared with the other. It was three in the morning but Poppy rang the eye SR at home. 'I know it's rare but I'm worried about a retrobulbar haemorrhage,' she told him.

'I'll be fifteen minutes.' To her relief, he took

her fears seriously. 'In the meantime, set up an
IV line and give mannitol 200mg, acetazolam-
ide 200mg and methylpred 250,' he said briskly.
'And let the surgeons know, though I suspect
they'll want to leave the malar a few days.'

By the time the registrar arrived Poppy had
administered the drugs, taken basic blood tests,
spoken with the surgeons and organised an on-
call interpreter to relieve the burden on Mr
Ullah's son.

Even in the short time that had elapsed since
Poppy had examined her patient his visual acu-
ity had deteriorated further, and after he'd
examined him the registrar said, 'We'll operate
immediately.' Within minutes he was on his
way to Theatre.

The following morning after she finished her
shift—and after another self-conscious, fraught
two minutes handing over to Tom—Poppy
visited Jamie as usual. He'd still not regained
consciousness and after three days the ICU team
had performed a tracheotomy so that the ventilator fed directly into a tube in his neck. He
was now also receiving food intravenously and
there'd already been one scare when he'd
developed an infection from the line that carried
the food, but fortunately he'd recovered
quickly.

'He took some breaths.' Kathleen, Jamie's mother, spent her nights in a chair by his bed, and she greeted Poppy with a pale smile. In the last two weeks she'd lost a lot of weight and there were deep strain lines engraved around her eyes and mouth, making her look years older than the twenty-eight that Poppy knew her to be. 'They're trying to wean him off the respirator again.'

But they'd tried before and Poppy had learned to tone down her enthusiasm; the general outlook now was pessimistic. 'I'm glad,' she said quietly. 'What did the physio think?'

'She was quite pleased.' Jamie was receiving physio every few hours to keep his chest clear and his limbs supple. 'She had him sitting up again last night.'

'Good.' Sitting, or rather being propped, up was important to maintain Jamie's sense of balance while he was unconscious. 'How's Anna?'

'Still naughty.' Kathleen grimaced. 'I'm sure you're right that it's just that she's missing all the attention. Rod's taking her to the zoo today, like you suggested. Perhaps that will help.'

'I hope so.' Jamie's nurse was waiting to sponge him and Poppy stood. 'I'll be back tomorrow. Try and get a rest today while they're out. You'll get sick yourself if you're too exhausted.'

'I know.' She pushed her hair wearily away from her face. Then, as Poppy was about to walk away, she said, 'We haven't thanked you. For all your help and. . .everything. You and Mr Grainger. We've been meaning to but. . .'

'I understand.' Poppy squeezed her hand, feeling the tears prickling behind her own eyes as she saw them forming in Kathleen's. 'I'm just so sorry for everything.'

'Whatever happens. . .' Kathleen was sobbing now. 'Whatever happens, I want you to know how grateful—'

'I know.' Poppy hugged her. 'Come and have a cup of tea,' she said shakily. 'My treat.'

'Thanks.' Kathleen wiped her eyes with the back of her hand as she looked back at her frail son. 'But I like to help with his bath. I think he enjoys it.'

Poppy washed her hands, took off the gown she'd worn to protect Jamie against any germs on her clothes, and left the unit. Outside she dabbed at her damp eyes with a tissue, then blew her nose.

She didn't hear anybody approaching and when Tom tilted her chin up she started, then swallowed heavily, embarrassed that he'd caught her like this. 'Jamie's unchanged,' she said huskily.

He released her. 'And Kathleen?'

'Coping.' Poppy pocketed the tissue. 'Just.'

'I came here, looking for you,' Tom said, surprising her. 'One of the eye consultants told me you saved a man's eyesight on Wednesday by diagnosing a retrobulbar haemorrhage.'

'Oh.' Poppy flushed. 'Oh, I was about to go and see how he was getting on. I'm glad they caught him in time.'

'*You* caught him in time.' He was so solemn that she tingled. 'Most of the time it's not thought of and the diagnosis is only made when the eye goes blind. Well done.'

She moistened her dry lips. 'Th-thank you,' she said shakily, deciding she found it easier to deal with his anger than his approval.

'I saw your application for the surgical rotation,' he continued. 'Your interview's scheduled for the Wednesday after Easter.'

Five weeks away. Poppy frowned. 'But they haven't even announced the short-list.'

'You're on it. You'll be told officially in a week.'

'Oh.' Her eyes flickered, confused now— pleased, but confused. She hadn't expected any help from him with this and now he was giving her an extra week to prepare. Did that mean that she had his support after all? How did he feel, then, about her being around for the next three years? She'd assumed that he wouldn't want that. 'And Derek?'

'Also short-listed. I've told him as well.' He pushed open the ICU doors, then looked back to where she still stood. 'That's all I can do for either of you. The selections will be completely impartial.'

'I know.' She managed a smile. 'Thanks.'

Almost a month later, Easter Sunday dawned unexpectedly warm and clear, and Poppy was singing tunelessly along with the Honda's radio as she turned up her parents' Oxford street. She signalled, waved to one of the neighbours, turned into the driveway and immediately slammed on the brakes, biting her tongue in the panic of smashing into the back of Tom's car.

The front door opened and her mother flew out. 'I heard the noise...' She frowned worriedly. 'Oh, Poppy, you didn't.'

'Only a little.' Poppy bent worriedly over the two bumpers. Hers had a slight dent which might or might not be new, but Tom's was unharmed. 'It was the sun and the shadow, and I wasn't expecting a car...' She frowned. 'What's he doing here, anyway?'

'Enjoying your mother's cooking,' Tom said calmly, striding towards them. He didn't seem particularly alarmed or surprised about her driving into his car. 'Hello, Poppy.'

'Hello.' She squinted at him, liking the shorts that left several inches of hard, muscled thigh exposed—liking, too, the casual khaki shirt, its sleeves rolled up to reveal strong forearms. Although she'd been working afternoons this last week and had seen quite a bit of him at work, the meetings had been frustratingly impersonal. This was the first time she'd seen him away from the hospital since that last night at his home.

Her mother said, 'When you told me again last week that Tom was busy for Easter I thought I'd call anyway. He promised straight away to change all his plans to. . .' She wrinkled her nose at her guest. 'What was it you were doing, Tom? Poppy did say but I forget—'

'I said he'd be working,' Poppy said sharply.

'You must have misread the roster,' Tom said smoothly, his narrowed gaze suggesting that her mother had already mentioned her excuse. 'I'm the consultant, remember?'

How could she forget? Frowning, Poppy walked past him and into the house, worried about what her father and Jeremy might have been saying in her absence. Her youthful crush on Tom had been the family joke for years. 'Where are the others?'

'In the garden.' Her mother took her arm

and steered her through the house. 'We've been enjoying the sun.'

Over an enormous roast lunch her mother had prepared Jeremy confirmed Poppy's fear that the family had been talking about her. 'Tom and I hunted out our old med-school year-books yesterday,' he said airily, his teasing eyes fixed on Poppy. 'Took ages to find them. Believe it or not, they were tucked away in the attic amongst *your* things.'

She paled. 'Really?' she said croakily. 'How strange.'

'That's what we thought.' He was grinning now and he wasn't the only one. They all were—even Tom.

'So what?' she said bravely, deciding that the only possible course was to meet them head on. She could hardly pretend that it hadn't been she who'd cut out every picture of Tom she'd been able to find—even though it had meant damaging Jeremy's year-books. 'I was very young.'

Jeremy and her father laughed out loud. 'What I want to know is what you did with them,' Jeremy said, wiping his eyes and exchanging a teasing look with his smiling friend. 'There must have been at least fifty pictures missing. Where the hell did you put them?'

'I made a scrapbook.'

That provoked general hilarity, during which she studied her cauliflower cheese. 'May we see it?' demanded her brother when he could finally talk.

Poppy narrowed her eyes fiercely. He was supposed to be an adult now, not a teasing child. Wouldn't he ever grow up? 'No.'

'But, Poppy, we'd love to see it,' her mother protested laughingly. 'I'm sure Tom would too, wouldn't you, Tom?'

'Very much,' he said easily.

'Too bad.' Stiffly she picked up her knife and fork again. 'Now if you've all finished laughing at me the food's getting cold.'

But she was the only one who started eating. 'Sorry, old man,' said Jeremy, still grinning at Tom. 'We knew she had a bit of a crush on you but if I'd known how bad it was I'd never have asked you to look after her.'

Tom said, 'I didn't mind.'

That brought Poppy's head up sharply. 'You knew?'

'I could hardly miss it,' he teased. 'All those long, soulful looks and, of course, there was that night you broke into my flat and took all your clothes off.'

'What?' Her parents' simultaneous roars and Jeremy's shout of laughter drowned her own feeble gasp.

'Poppy, you didn't,' cried her mother, obviously appalled. 'Poor Tom. How on earth did you get rid of her?'

'Mother!'

Ignoring Poppy's indignant squeal, Tom grinned. 'It wasn't too difficult,' he said easily. 'I did the "I like you but in a brotherly way" routine. Worked at the time.'

'Thank God for that.' Her father looked relieved. 'With those books she used to read I'm surprised you got away unscathed.'

'For your information,' Poppy said stiffly, shouting to be heard over their amusement and glaring at each of them in turn until they quietened, 'I am not some sort of voracious sexual deviant.' Keeping her gaze very firmly averted from Tom she continued, '*Most* people would be kind enough not to find my teenage crush the biggest joke of the decade, and *most* families would show a little more support.'

Hoping that she'd shamed them into at least a semblance of good behaviour, she sliced into her meat. To her relief, they all began eating again and the rest of the meal passed reasonably smoothly, although every time she looked up and saw Tom she flushed.

Afterwards, Jeremy was called up to the hospital and her parents shooed Poppy and Tom into the garden while they did the dishes. Tom

sat on the grass beside her deckchair, bracing
his back against one side of it. In celebration
of the warm day she was wearing a short skirt,
and his hair brushed her knee so enticingly that
she had to grip her hands tight to stop herself
touching it. 'Why didn't you tell me you were
coming?'

'Why didn't you pass on the invitation?'

She closed her eyes. Warm sun. Full tummy.
Tom. This was paradise. 'I didn't think you'd
be interested.'

He tipped his head back, rubbing it from side
to side against her knee so that the warm slide
of his hair teased her thigh. 'I like your family.'

'Just not me,' she said dully.

His head shook against her leg. 'Maybe if
you hadn't dented my car.'

Poppy's eyes snapped open. 'But I didn't—'
His teasing grin stopped her protest. 'See if
you find this so funny,' she grated, grinding a
handful of her father's newly mown grass into
his shiny hair with the heel of her hand.

She leapt away, tossing a few sods of earth
vaguely in his direction as she raced for the
porch. But she'd forgotten his rugby prowess.
He was far faster than she, and his flying tackle
caught her off balance, tumbling her onto the
lawn.

'You great...bully,' she said through

clenched teeth, rolling over and struggling and kicking against his laughing triumph. 'I'll be bruised all over tomorrow.'

'Then be still.' He pressed her into the grass while he captured her wrists with one strong hand and held them behind her head. 'And apologise.'

She wriggled fiercely but he was too strong for her and his eyes gleamed a vivid, triumphant blue when she finally quietened. 'Sorry, Tom, I'll never throw dirt at you again,' he prompted.

Poppy gritted her teeth. 'Sorry, Tom, I'll never throw dirt at you again.'

'Good girl.' He tapped her nose and as she stared up into his face with wide eyes, absorbing the heat of him, the rough rub of the arm that held her captured and his spicy clean male scent, his finger brushed her mouth and sent a pulse of heat shivering along her nerves.

Abruptly he levered himself away from her. He took her hand and lifted her up, too, and she stood mutely while he brushed little fragments of grass from her clothes. 'I might have ruined this,' he said roughly, his thumb rubbing at a green stain that marred her pale skirt along the line of her hip where the impact of him had thrown her forward onto the lawn.

'It'll wash out.' Her heart was beating so fast

that she could feel it quivering in her chest. 'It's cotton.'

'Cotton?' His voice was so low that it rumbled like an earthquake across her senses. 'Is this cotton, too?' One impatient hand tugged her T-shirt free of the waistband of her skirt, then lingered at the loosened edge, his fingers twisting restlessly in the fabric.

'Yes.' She could barely speak.

'Are you wearing anything under it?' he demanded raggedly.

'Nothing.'

His eyes watching the house behind her, he slid his hand beneath the shirt—onto the warmth of her hip, up along the curve of her waist and then captured her breast, his thumb nudging the tightness of her nipple.

He murmured his approval at her gasp, catching her as she wavered limply in the air—her body too awash with sensation to stay upright.

But after one brief torturing caress he released her again, meeting her dazed stare with tight determination. 'No. They'll see us.'

'I don't care.'

'I do.' The mouth she'd been studying compressed as he straightened her. 'Poppy Brown, you really are the most wanton creature.'

'Am I?' Poppy brightened. 'Really?'

He sighed. 'Really.' He turned her towards

the house and slapped her bottom. 'Inside, minx.'

To Poppy's irritation, she didn't get him to herself again before Jeremy arrived back, and then he and Tom went off to meet up with some of their old medical school colleagues, without inviting her along.

His embraces had left her confused and impatient, longing to talk with him again. Had he changed his mind about her? She stayed until eight, hoping that they'd be back, but they weren't and she couldn't delay her return any longer.

Although Easter Sunday and Monday were public holidays and Tom was going fishing with Jeremy the next day, junior staff such as she worked normal rostered shifts and she was scheduled to start night duty at eleven.

On Tuesday morning Tom hadn't arrived by eight when she finished her shift and she trudged home to her flat. She didn't want to sleep. Her interview was the next day and she needed to do some preparation, but the night had been too busy and she ended up in bed.

It felt as if she'd merely dozed for an hour when loud banging on the door roused her, but a sleepy glance at her bedside clock showed that she'd been asleep all afternoon.

When she opened the door Tom strode inside, not bothering to wait for an invitation. 'What if I'd been the burglar?' he demanded, his face set in a scowl. 'Don't you ever learn?'

CHAPTER ELEVEN

POPPY's mouth was still open and she lifted her hair away from her face with one shaking hand and blinked vaguely at Tom.

'Never, *never* open your door without checking who it is,' he added sharply. 'Understand?'

She shook her head. 'T-Tom. . .?'

'It's Jamie.' Suddenly he grinned. He grinned and she melted. 'He's conscious. Over the Easter break. I thought you'd want to know.'

'Conscious?' Poppy's head was spinning. 'Is he. . .all right?'

'He wanted his kite and his mother,' he told her. 'In that order. The consensus is that he's going to be fine.'

'Thank goodness.' She sagged against the door.

'Get dressed.' His gaze flickered over her pyjamas dismissively. 'I'll take you to see him. Kathleen wanted you to come.'

'This is Dr Brown,' Kathleen told Jamie when she and Tom arrived—a new, revitalised Kathleen now that the dark shadows and lines around her face had faded. 'Jamie, do you remember Dr Brown?'

He shook his head and Poppy wasn't surprised. The amount of trauma he'd had would have erased the memory of those hours before he'd lost consciousness. But Jamie still smiled. 'Hi!' His voice was raspy and dry but bright.

'Hi, yourself.' She crouched beside him.

'You don't look like a doctor.'

She smiled. 'What do doctors look like?'

'Like him.' Jamie grinned at Tom, a slightly lopsided grin that made her worry a little about nerve damage. 'He's my friend. Is he your friend too?'

She exchanged a brief look with Tom and judged from his guarded expression that the answer to that was not simple. 'He's my boss,' she said lightly.

'Does that mean you're getting married?'

'No.' Poppy's face felt like thick concrete. 'No, it doesn't mean that.' She darted him a quick look. 'He's too old and grumpy for me,' she said sweetly.

'Oh.' Jamie looked disappointed. 'I've been sick.'

'Yes, I know.' Refusing to look at Tom, although she sensed him glowering at her, Poppy studied the equipment around the bed. Jamie had been disconnected from everything but an ordinary intravenous line.

'Now I'm better.'

'Now you won't stop talking, you mean.' His father grinned and when Jamie grinned too Poppy saw that their smiles were mirror images of each other and she relaxed, chiding herself for not being more observant. The asymmetry of Jamie's smile had nothing to do with his head injury.

'Sorry, Poppy, Tom,' said Jamie's father. 'He does rabbit on.' He draped an arm around his wife's shoulders. 'Not that we're complaining, mind.'

'When can I go home?' asked Jamie. 'Tomorrow?'

'When your doctor says so.' Judging from his incredible progress, Poppy suspected that that wouldn't be long.

'When the doctors are sick of you, more like.' Kathleen rolled her eyes at Poppy and Tom. 'Once he's off that drip there'll be no stopping him,' she said happily.

'We'll look forward to that.' Poppy stood up, smiling a farewell. 'Bye, Jamie. See you tomorrow.'

He waved. 'Bye.'

Tom looked at her irritably as they washed their hands. When they left the unit he caught her waist and forced her roughly against the wall of the deserted corridor. 'Old and grumpy, am I?' he growled, silencing her delighted giggle with his mouth. 'Witch.'

The sound of something heavy being dropped startled them apart, and then Tom groaned and Poppy looked up and met Lucy's and Kim's astonished gazes with horror.

'Sorry,' said Lucy faintly, bending to retrieve the notes she'd obviously just dropped. 'We didn't mean to. . .'

'Interrupt.' Kim spoke mechanically, her eyes almost as wide as her open mouth. 'Um. . . hi, Poppy.'

'Hi.' Poppy cleared her throat. 'We were just. . .'

'Celebrating.' Tom sighed. 'Jamie Turner's woken up. We were celebrating.'

'And why not?' Lucy was suddenly brisk. 'Why not, indeed?' With a fixed smile she took Kim's arm and drew her away. 'Come along, Kim. Back to work.'

Tom grimaced. 'That's done it,' he said softly. 'Both our reputations shattered.'

'Don't you mind?'

She'd expected him to be furious but his shrug was philosophical. 'Had to happen sooner or later.' His hand curved around her chin as he leant closer. 'With you involved, it was never going to stay a secret.'

But Poppy stopped him, one hand flat against his chest. 'When you say involved,' she said huskily, 'does that mean involved, involved?'

He stilled. 'I want to make love to you. I thought that's what you wanted, too.'

She stepped away from him, holding herself very stiff and very straight. 'You told me you wanted order in your life,' she said, keeping her eyes fixed on the perfectly symmetrical knot of his tie. 'You said you wanted calm. You said I'd drive you mad. Has something changed that?'

'Those things are still true,' he said wryly. 'But I'll compromise. I've missed you. Life's seemed too quiet this past month without seeing you properly.'

'So now you want me in your life?'

'Poppy, stop rushing things,' he growled. 'This isn't a proposal.'

She stiffened. 'You're suggesting an affair?'

'A *relationship*.' He took her hand. 'Don't be in such a hurry; give us time to get to know each other.'

Give him time to *get her out of his system*, she substituted, remembering him using those words once before. She tugged her hand free and asked, 'How long is this *relationship* supposed to last?'

'I don't know.' He was frowning. 'A few months. Perhaps longer.'

Perhaps longer. 'I don't think so.' She

studied him, loving him but knowing that she couldn't bear waiting to see if she earned that 'perhaps'. 'I don't think that's what I want.'

And she left him there. And as she walked back to her flat she realised that for the first time in her life she felt old. Old and cynical.

Poppy's interview the next afternoon was the last for the rotation. It was scheduled for three-thirty but she wasn't shown in until four. The Professor of Surgery who was leading the interviews apologised heartily for the delay, then welcomed her and introduced her to the panel— the Prof, four other hospital surgeons, a medical staffing officer and Tom.

Briefly she met Tom's impassive gaze, then looked quickly away with her fists clenched, forcing herself to concentrate. The panel ran through her CV and asked about her interests. Then someone said, 'I see you're from Oxford, Dr Brown. Any relation to Malcolm Brown?'

'He's my father.'

The surgeon who'd asked the question beamed. 'I know him well. He's done an enormous amount for the college. You're not inclined towards ENT yourself?'

'Trauma,' Poppy said flatly. 'My interest is trauma.'

Tom might have been expected to question

her then but he said nothing and instead the Professor said, 'Your referees have all remarked on your medical and interpersonal skills, Poppy. Although confident you'll succeed in whichever field you choose, some have expressed regret that you've not elected a career in medicine or general practice.'

'I enjoy medicine,' she admitted, 'and patient contact and primary care are important to me, but my career interest is surgery.'

As time and the questions progressed Poppy grew more and more tense about Tom's silence. He was the only one not to have asked anything, and if it was obvious to her it must be doubly so to the rest of the panel.

She hadn't expected overt encouragement from him, but his lack of questions was highly discouraging and the thought that her refusal to have an affair with him might jeopardise her career shocked her deeply.

At the end of the interview the Professor thanked her and escorted her out of the room, explaining that the results would be announced at six—after which there'd be an opportunity for each candidate, successful or otherwise, to meet with the panel to discuss his or her performance.

Poppy went directly to McDonald's where she knew the other candidates were waiting.

Fifteen of them had been short-listed for the interview but only six were required for the rotation.

'I can't believe they asked you about your father,' Derek complained when she told them about her session. 'I thought that sort of thing wasn't allowed—it's so old-school. Guaranteed you'll get in.'

'Absolutely guaranteed,' one of the others said.

'You think?' Poppy doubted that her father's position made any difference, and she knew that Tom's obvious disapproval would counter-balance any other factors in her favour. 'Doing the casualty run's supposed to be the best way in, isn't it?'

'Fingers crossed.' Derek looked gloomy. 'My father sells cars. If it's "old-school" I'm sunk.'

But at six they discovered that it was Derek, not Poppy, who'd made the grade, along with five others. 'Congratulations,' she said quietly, genuinely pleased for him.

'Poppy, I'm sorry.' Derek looked distraught. 'I'd hoped we'd be working together again.'

'Never mind,' she said stiffly.

'Wait!' he said urgently when she turned away. 'Talk to them. It might have been something simple—perhaps they want you to get the first part of your exams first.'

'It's not a requirement,' she answered vaguely, tugging her arm free. Then she hesitated. 'Derek, did Tom ask you any questions at the interview?'

Derek looked puzzled. 'Of course. Lots. Why?'

'Nothing.' Poppy's head dropped. 'Well done. Go and celebrate.'

She trudged distractedly through the hospital and out into the car park, frowning at the traffic that swerved angrily around her as she meandered across the road. It was still early, still light, but once inside her horrible flat there seemed little else to do but go to bed.

She curled into a ball beneath her duvet and lay dry-eyed and shocked. She didn't know Tom at all. The man she'd fallen in love with hadn't been there today. That had been a hard, cold man she never wanted to see again.

Somehow, sometime, she must have slept because she was startled awake by shouting and banging on her door. 'Poppy! Poppy, I know you're there.'

Still half-asleep, she dragged herself out of bed and trudged through the lounge. 'Is that the burglar?'

'Fruit cake! Open the door.'

She froze. 'I'm in bed.'

'I'll break it down.'

'You paid for it,' she said flatly. 'Do what you like.'

She heard him swear. 'I've got your horrible suit,' he said tersely. 'Let me in or I'll dump it in an incinerator.'

Her suit? Curiosity seeping through her misery, she unclamped the locks. 'Where was it?'

'A spare locker. In Theatres.' Tom pushed past her and dumped her precious suit on the couch. 'The nurses say it's been there for weeks. Finally the cleaner mentioned it to someone in Security and they matched it with your ridiculous drawing. Sweeny bleeped me.'

He was frowning at her and when she walked closer to look at her suit he caught her arm, twisting her towards him. His thumbs brushed her cheeks and they were damp and she realised that she must have been crying after all.

'Poppy, I'm sorry.'

'I put it in a locker,' she said faintly, her eyes fixed on the suit. 'I remember I put it in a locker and then when I came out of Theatre I forgot. I thought it had been stolen.'

'You didn't come and talk to the panel after the jobs were announced.'

She frowned. 'Security must think I'm an idiot.'

He smoothed her hair. 'Not getting on

the rotation's not such a bad thing.'

'What about my shoes?'

'In my car. Poppy, if you're still determined to join the programme we're taking on another group of doctors in February. You could reapply.'

'Where's my drawing?'

'Security wanted to keep it.' He sighed. 'Try something different for six months. Applications are still open for obstetric and paediatric and medical SHOs. Broaden your experience while you've got the chance.'

'Why did they want to keep it?'

Tom sighed. He tucked his finger under her chin, forcing her to meet his steady gaze. 'Poppy, talk to me.'

'Are they laughing at the drawing?'

'Probably,' he admitted. 'It's pretty odd.'

She swallowed heavily. 'I was never any good at art.'

'It doesn't matter.' With a muffled curse he pulled her into his arms. His hand stroked soothingly down her back. 'I'm sorry you're unhappy about not getting a job. The standard of the applicants was very high. Your references and grades are excellent but you were the only short-listed candidate who hadn't either already sat for part one exams or was about to. The panel worried about how committed you were.'

'I'll find something.' She sniffed, twisting her head aside rather than letting it burrow into his shirt. 'I think I'll go to Aberdeen.'

He drew back, blinking at her. 'Aberdeen?'

'There's a good rotation there I might try for. It's still being advertised.'

'You want to go to Scotland?'

'I've never been. I like porridge.'

His hand twisted in her hair pulled her head gently back. 'That's not a good enough reason to go and live there,' he said softly. 'Scotland's wild and beautiful and you must visit but I can make you porridge.'

'I'm not staying,' she said stiffly. 'I can't change the way I am. I'll never be calm and controlled and elegant. I'll never be a Janet DeBeer.'

'Thank God for that.' He looked appalled. 'Poppy—'

'No, Tom.' Poppy pulled away from him and sat herself stiffly on the arm of the couch, her eyes fixed firmly on a purple flower woven into the red carpet at her feet. 'Let me finish.' She drew a deep shuddering breath. 'You were right, I think, today. I don't think you were fair, or ethical, but you were right. I can't stay here. I can't keep seeing you every day.' She met his eyes. 'I'm glad I didn't get the job.'

'But I didn't. . .' His brow darkened. 'You

think I rigged the interview?'

'Your opinion was obvious.'

'You have no idea.' He strode to the window and braced his arms against the frame, his tone fierce. 'You have no bloody idea what I was going through,' he said furiously.

'You didn't say anything.'

'Because I'd already declared my conflict of interest to the others,' he snapped. 'The agreement was that I neither questioned you nor voted.'

She was frowning. 'Conflict of interest?'

'The sweet irony of the whole mess was that all along I knew the job wouldn't be right for you,' he said bitterly. 'I knew it wouldn't be right but I wanted you to do well. I even hoped they'd vote for you but I sure as hell didn't do anything unethical.'

Poppy stood up and shook her head, bewildered. 'Tom, you haven't told me what you meant——'

'Poppy, listen to me.' He was gentler now. 'I've seen you working, I've heard how you think about medicine and I know you'd make a fabulous GP. Surgery would stifle you. You've been swayed by your family and you haven't considered your options enough.'

Her hands were trembling. 'General practice?'

'Or medicine, or psychiatry, or paediatrics,' he said softly. 'Try them all. If you still want surgery then come back to it—it won't go away.'

She closed her eyes. In a lot of ways he made sense—was voicing doubts she'd had herself. 'You said there are still vacancies for paediatric and medical SHOs here. You mean at the National?'

'Yes, at the National.' He came to her, took her hands and guided her to the couch. 'Try one of them, Poppy. Afterwards, if you're still interested in surgery, you'll have my full support. You know I'm never going to sway an interview or abuse my influence, but I will support you.'

Oh. She frowned. He wanted her to stay at the National? 'You said. . .you said before that the panel wouldn't let you question me. But you interviewed Derek. Why not me?'

Tom was very still. 'You know why not you.'

'B-because you're biased?'

His mouth quirked. '*Extremely* biased.'

'You wanted me to go away because I wouldn't. . .have an affair with you,' she said faintly.

He lifted one shoulder. 'Not good for my ego,' he admitted wryly. 'But let's just say I haven't given up all hope.'

'I won't, you know.' Poppy backed away fractionally, not liking the predatory gleam in his eyes. 'Stay away from me.'

Tom laughed, still coming towards her. 'Why? Frightened you might change your mind?'

She held out her arms to fend off his advance. 'Stop it.'

'You told me once that you'd love me if I was nice to you.' He tilted his head, teasing her. 'I can be nice to you.'

'I lied.' Poppy backed more. 'Go away.'

He grinned. 'I'll stop if you show me your scrapbook.'

Poppy sucked in her cheeks, cursing Jeremy. 'I was very young when I made it.' She let her arms drop, then crossed her fingers behind her back. 'I don't love you, you know.'

'Show it to me.'

'I lost it.'

'Poppy. . .'

She lifted her chin. 'It doesn't mean anything.' But his face was determined and she sighed. The scrapbook was a remnant of her adolescence; it would hurt but perhaps it was time she destroyed it. Without another word she went to her bedroom, reached under the mattress and retrieved it. 'Don't laugh.'

'I won't.' His face was solemn but when he

took the battered book from her hands she saw his eyes twinkle. 'I promise.'

They sat on the bed, Poppy silently shaking with nerves as he opened it and studied the photographs she'd displayed so lovingly. After looking at a couple he said, 'When was this?'

'In my first term at St John's. I came to watch you play rugby. You didn't see me.'

He flicked through a few more pages filled with the pictures she'd taken of him during that year and then looked up, obviously perturbed. 'Poppy, you never said anything.'

She smiled sadly. 'Would it have made any difference?'

'It might if you'd told me.'

'To you I was just Jeremy's irritating kid sister who couldn't keep her mouth shut.'

'To me you were Jeremy's *sexy* kid sister,' he countered, his voice very deep, 'although I won't argue about the mouth.'

Poppy's mouth dropped open. 'I was *sexy*?'

'*Very* sexy.' His mouth quirked. 'You were wanton even then. All big green eyes, luscious hair and pert little breasts naked in my bed.'

'But you sent me away.'

'You were very young and you were my friend's sister.' He tapped her nose. 'And after promising Jeremy I could hardly—' He stopped. 'Of course I sent you away,' he said abruptly. 'It wouldn't have been right to do anything else.'

But Poppy had caught the words he'd tried to stop. 'What did any of that have to do with Jeremy?' she demanded.

Tom's attention was back on her scrapbook. 'Nothing. Forget it. You were too young and you needed to concentrate on passing your exams.'

Poppy swallowed heavily. Too nervous to probe further, she looked down at the pictures. 'Did you ever think of me afterwards?'

'From time to time.' He turned the next page. 'When I saw your name on the new casualty intake I admit I did speculate a little.'

She remembered Lucy saying he'd been 'thoughtful'. She took a deep breath. 'When you saw me again. . .did you think I was still sexy?'

Tom looked at her. 'Incredibly.'

While she stared at him, her eyes wide as plates, he returned to her scrapbook. He pointed to a thin photograph. 'When was this?'

'That was the week before you finished your houseman year,' she told him numbly. 'You and Jeremy were going out. I sneaked the picture from my bedroom window.'

'Why is it cut like this?'

She flushed. 'I chopped out your date. Some busty blonde.'

He smiled. 'You were jealous.'

She turned the next page quickly, avoiding his gaze. 'This is your graduation.' Her forehead wrinkled as she studied the woman next to him. 'Look, I didn't realise before, there's Janet DeBeer beside you.' Poppy scowled at the histopathologist's besotted expression. 'She's practically all over you.'

But instead of studying the picture he was grinning at her. 'Poppy, I presume you have grasped the fact that you're the most beautiful woman in the world to me?'

Poppy opened her mouth but no sound came out. She blinked but her vision was still blurred. She tried to breathe but her chest was locked tight. Needing air, she struggled off the bed, then the room spun, her ears roared and she slid to the floor.

Tom was holding her legs in the air when she came to, and when he saw that her eyes were open he lowered them gently to the floor and crouched beside her. 'I suppose that means no?'

'Yes.' Her voice was a croak. 'No.'

He lifted her up and laid her on the bed, stretching out beside her and resting his head on one bent elbow. 'When you were sixteen I thought you were sweet,' he said lightly, one finger tracing the line of her breastbone. 'When you were eighteen you were delicious.'

'A-and now I'm twenty-five?'

'Irresistible.' He kissed the curve of her cheek beneath her eye and she couldn't breathe again. 'I tried to fight it. You're still too young for me, you're inexperienced, I know I should give you more time but you've turned my life upside down and I can't keep away any longer. I love you.'

She wriggled up. 'You love me?' It was a squeak.

'Yes.' He took her hand and pressed his mouth to her palm. 'I love your maddening mind. I love your openness, your brazenness, your lateness, your silliness, your grouchiness. I love the funny way you suck in your cheeks. I love your freckles. I love you passionately, madly. . .' he lowered his mouth to her throat '. . .besottedly. I adore you.'

'I do, too,' she gasped. 'I mean, not me, I don't love me—I love you. Tom, I. . .love you.' She fell back onto the bed, laughing, her arms outstretched. 'I love you. I love you. I love—' Poppy sat up. 'You definitely told me I'd drive you mad.'

'Yes.' He was grinning. 'With desire.' But he saw her scepticism and laughed. 'All right, you'll make my life hell,' he admitted. 'But you can do what you want—crash my car, set fire to the garden, mess up my kitchen—I don't care any more.'

'I'll probably do all those things,' she confessed, lifting her mouth for his kiss. 'Tom, you're not making sense. Yesterday you said you only wanted an affair.'

'No. I said I wasn't proposing.'

He kissed her again, a light, teasing kiss but she twisted away. 'That's the same thing.'

'No, it isn't.' Overcoming her puny resistance, he nuzzled her ear. 'You're inexperienced and you're young. I don't want to rush you. You need time to get to know me, decide what you really want. What I meant yesterday was that we'll spend a few months together, perhaps longer, and decide what we want to do after that.'

She pulled her head back. 'I didn't understand.'

'I only worked that out later.' He smiled at her surprise. 'For God's sake, Poppy, I couldn't keep my hands off you. Any other woman—' He stopped and his mouth twisted ruefully. 'Let's just say I thought it was obvious how I felt,' he finished flatly. One hand slid beneath her jacket. 'How I'm feeling now.'

She captured the hand and guided it to

her breast. 'I thought you wanted sex.'

'I do.' He cupped her, his thumb rubbing softly back and forth—catching at her nipple and making her restless. He saw her squirm and smiled. 'And you do too. I thought you were angry because I wasn't going to propose immediately. I was giving you time to cool down.'

Poppy stiffened. 'Tom, I love you.'

He pushed up her jacket, baring her breasts completely. 'I love you, too.'

She gasped when his mouth tugged at her nipple, her body softening again, but this was important and she tried to resist—tried to think. 'I want to marry you.'

Tom's laugh was muffled against her heated flesh. 'I want that too, minx.' He groaned, then gathered her closer, tumbling her beneath him onto the sheets. 'I'd marry you tomorrow if I was sure you knew what you were doing.' He cupped her bottom. 'Which you don't.' One hand went to the button that fastened her pyjama bottoms. 'God, I want you.'

Poppy twined her legs around him, arching and feeling herself burning. 'Actually, I know exactly what I want.'

'Good.' He groaned his satisfaction when the button released. He tugged the bottoms down to bare her thighs. 'Very good.'

'And I can't wait to be a virgin bride.'

Tom froze. Slowly he lifted his head. 'You are a witch,' he said softly, blue eyes gleaming pure sapphire flame as he inspected her flushed determination. 'You expect me to give in to cheap blackmail like that?'

She slid one daring hand down his muscled chest and paused at the fastening of his belt, loving the sharp intake of breath that disclosed his desire. 'About marriage,' she whispered. 'It's not the technicality—it's the principle.'

Tom's eyes narrowed and she knew that he remembered using those words himself. 'You want me to accept that you know your own mind,' he said heavily.

'I'm all grown up, Tom.' She smiled. 'I love your protectiveness and your chivalry, but I'm not Jeremy's little sister any more. I'm a full grown woman and I'm not going to change my mind. I want you for ever.'

He lowered his head and for one taut minute, then two, there was silence but when he looked at her again she saw his acceptance. 'You're right,' he said flatly. 'You're all grown up. It's just taken me some time to get used to it.'

'I love you so much.' She was laughing as he came back to her, laughing and crying, and he was laughing too and he was heavy and wonderful. 'Make love to me, Tom.'

'Yes.' But instead of deepening their embrace he paused, his head still against her breast. Then, abruptly, he tugged up her pyjama bottoms, pulled down her top and eased himself away, capturing the urgent hands she lifted to stop him and raising them to his mouth for a tender kiss. 'After the wedding.'

Poppy gasped, appalled. She struggled up onto her elbows. 'But I just meant. . . Tom, I wasn't serious!'

'But you were right.' He kissed her nose and then her lips, a gentle, teasing caress that did nothing to assuage her need, lifting his head away easily when she tried to force him back. 'You were right. This is too special to rush. I want to wait until we're married.'

Laughing at her frustrated squeaks, he rolled away from her and stood up. He hauled her easily to her feet, evading her seeking arms as she tried to open his shirt. 'Poppy Brown, you really are a wanton hussy. I said no!'

'Think of it as casual sex,' she protested. 'A final fling before marriage.'

'I don't need one.' He scooped her into his arms, carried her into the bathroom, lifted her into the bath, turned on the shower and held her there, laughing at her shrieks as the cold water seeped through her pyjamas and soaked them both. 'Marriage,' he pronounced hoarsely, 'is going to be perfect.'

MEDICAL ROMANCE™

Large Print

Titles for the next six months...

April

INCURABLY ISABELLE	Lilian Darcy
A HEART OF GOLD	Jessica Matthews
FIRST THINGS FIRST	Josie Metcalfe
WINGS OF LOVE	Meredith Webber

May

WAIT AND SEE	Sharon Kendrick
TOO CLOSE FOR COMFORT	Jessica Matthews
SECOND CHANCE	Josie Metcalfe
DOCTOR DELICIOUS	Flora Sinclair

June

A VERY SPECIAL NEED	Caroline Anderson
A HEALING SEASON	Jessica Matthews
HAPPY CHRISTMAS, DOCTOR DEAR	
	Elisabeth Scott
A FATHER FOR CHRISTMAS	Meredith Webber

MEDICAL ROMANCE™

Large Print